Tracking Jane, Episode 1

A Novella by
Eduardo Suastegui

Shadow-7
Copyright © 2014, 2015, Eduardo Suastegui
Published by Eduardo Suastegui, Print edition, revision 1.51

Published By Eduardo Suastegui
A *Voice of the Mute Tales* production
http://eduardosuastegui.com

ISBN-13: 978-1516805709
ISBN-10: 1516805704

Acknowledgements

A story like this one could not even enter the imagination if not for the sacrifice of our men and women in uniform. To them and their families, I dedicate this book. And for those who came back alive, yet gravely injured, I pray for healing and restoration to the very way of life they gave so much to protect.

Chapter 1

In the back seat, Shady is stirring and whining. I may not give her much credit, but she's smarter than she acts most days. Sensitive, too, enough to tell we're getting close.

"Down, girl," I tell her, but she doesn't mind me, as usual.

Some of the boys back on base said it was because two "bees with itches" never get along. I should've reported that as sexual harassment to my CO. But I collected more satisfaction by popping the nose of the first and last jerk that said it to my face.

The Boulder, Colorado mountains around Eldorado Canyon State Park loom large, and I know I'm getting close, too. To another job. To another chase. To another chance to prove to the world and to myself that I'm really back, all the way back, a full up functioning member of this society I no longer understand and struggle not to hate.

Scraping at her seat now, Shady is getting louder.

"If you tear that seat, I swear I'll—"

Through the rear view mirror I see her eyes, attentive and fixed on me, as if to say, "What will you do to me, really?"

"Down, Shady girl," I tell her again, calling her by the name I'm sure she hates since I changed it.

She used to go by Shadow-19. When I trained her, I came to believe she didn't deserve that name, more so when she washed out of the program. I didn't think she deserved it when they gave her to me as a therapy dog, my consolation prize when I got back from my last tour. She's no Shadow, not like the Shadow I left behind to keep fighting the war that tore me up.

I'm sure Shady will do fine today, though,

like she did six months ago on a similar job not far from here, in Louisville, Colorado—that is, if this job turns out as I determined from the email I got from the police department. But truth is she doesn't deserve the name Shadow. Not when she couldn't find a pile of her own dung on most days, no matter how hard I've trained her.

Up ahead I see the dirt lot, now turned into a command center for the search and rescue operation. I see a lot of cars, some law enforcement, most civies, volunteers, probably. But I don't see a lot of bodies. I'm guessing the bulk of the search party's left already. That's fine. I prefer to track alone.

Shady near knocks me off my everyday legs when I open the back door of my SUV. I stumble a bit but still manage to grab on to her collar to put her on the leash. Together we walk to the back of my 4Runner, where I tether her to the tow hitch.

I take a minute to steady my legs, until I remember these aren't the ones that will carry me today.

I look around one more time. Doesn't seem like anyone's noticed my arrival. That's also fine. What I'm about to do is best done alone, too, though I ain't ashamed of doing it in public. In fact, I figure the more people that see it, the better. They need to face the consequences of their nice, comfy lives, even if I'm the one that has to live with the grand total of what protecting the American way of life took from me.

I push up the SUV's hatchback and sit on the lip of the trunk. After another look around, I roll my pant legs up to my knees. Now he appears. Out of the corner of my eye I see him, an officer striding toward me.

"You Jane McMurtry?" he's shouting as he approaches.

"As seen on TV and the Internet," I shout back.

I unlatch my left leg, slide off the sleeve, and just as he's a few steps away, I drop it on the trunk with a nice dramatic thump.

"Do you need a minute?" he says now, respectful voice and all.

"What do you think?"

"I'll come back."

"I do need a minute," I say. "That don't mean you can't watch if it turns you on."

He stops, takes a step to his right, puts his hands on his hips, looks away, and I'm hearing my mother's voice telling me I need to treat boys nicer.

"Trading my every day legs for my working ones," I say by way of ice breaker. By now I've released my right leg, which I deposit rather than drop next to the left one.

From a skinny, black duffel bag of sorts, I go to pull my other set, telling him, "And these are them, the ones I use for special assignments." I take one out, start working on the sleeve to ready it for mounting. "They're sturdier, a feat of engineering for sure. Easy to balance on, too. Better for long walks like the one we're about to take, but not so comfortable for everyday duty. Grind on you when you're driving, too, so ain't no way I was gonna wear them all the way clear down from Fort Collins."

He nods, drops his arms, still unsure what to do with them, and ends up stuffing his hands into the pockets of his long canvas shorts. I allow myself a second to notice his muscular, lean calves. Only a second, though, before I go back to the job at hand.

He takes two steps toward me. "Are those the ones you're training with? For the..." He clears his throat. "The Olympics?"

"Not for the *Special* Olympics, if that's what you almost asked."

Shady snorts at that, as if to back up my position on this particular matter.

I add, "I'm going for the real thing or none at all."

"Like that guy from South Africa. That..." Another clearing of the throat. "That Blade Runner. Ran the 400, I think."

"That he did," I reply. "On them bouncy legs. Mine ain't so blade-like, as you can see." I slap the right leg, now fully attached. "But yeah, these are them."

I start working on the left one. He waits for me, nice enough to stay quiet and not go on about the Olympics or mention all the buzz my Twitter feed's been getting about me going for it, first American to really try it, war veteran to boot, the kind of stuff my agent just loves, loves to brag about. Even if I'm just going for the shot put.

I stand up and take a couple of steps, hand out. "Now that I'm all back in one piece, as it were, Jane McMurtry at your service." I almost add "big boy," but think better of it, even though at my 6' 1", he still towers over me by a good two to three inches.

With a tepid smile, he says, "Deputy Murphy. Dan Murphy. Friends call me Danny."

"Ain't your friend yet," I reply as I squeeze his hand. "But Shady and I will be glad to make your acquaintance as we work the job."

"You from the south, Ms. McMurtry?"

"Nope. Just a Wyoming-Colorado hick."

"Hmm," he says, and I guess he's thinking

back to all them articles he's probably read on me. If so, he's read I'm an educated woman with an English degree plus all the training the Army could shove into me. "On the cusp of her master's degree," someone tweeted about me when proclaiming my education and intellectual prowess.

"That's right, Mr. Murphy. Just an ordinary hick. Don't believe all you read. Education don't make a man educated. Sometimes quite the opposite."

His frown suggests he doesn't appreciate that observation, like he's on the cusp of something educational himself.

I grin at what I aim to say next. "On the other hand, women stand a much better chance. They tend to latch on and capture more. Something anatomical, I'm sure a crackpot expert will tell us some day. This one here standing before you, though? All hick."

He points at Shady. "German Shepherd?"

"Twenty-four, seven, unfortunately."

"I thought they were the best."

For a moment, I consider whether to indulge yet another canine conversation, the kind where people go to picking my brain while spouting everything they think they already know.

"You Irish?" I ask him.

"About one fourth," he says.

"Me too, so we're making one of them connections already. Who knows? Friendship may be around the corner. I might even tell you what kind of beer I fancy."

He smiles at that.

Realizing I've been holding it all this time, I let go of his hand and step back to my SUV's trunk. After I stash my everyday legs in the duffel bag, I retrieve my backpack. Doing one last check, I unzip it to make sure I got all I need. It's packed for a one to two day hike. I'm not planning on it, but if I have to, in this weather, I can overnight it in the high country.

"You got your gear?" I ask him once I've hitched my bag on.

"Back at my car."

"Well, let's go, then." I lock my SUV and

take Shady's leash. I can tell she's about to lurch forward, so I tug back on her, saying, *"Pfallow."* She minds me, for once, Dutch command and all.

"You trained her in the Army," Murphy says. "Along with that other—"

"That's right." I cut him off before the conversation goes to Shadow, or before I have to tell him Shady never made the cut. I sure don't want to get into how Shady became a therapy dog at the VA, which she stunk at given her hyper temperament. And I don't want to say how or why she ended up with me, some therapist's bright idea to smooth my re-entry into civilian life.

"Which one's your car?" I ask before he has a chance to keep stoking his doggy curiosity.

He waves ahead at a white Tahoe with police markings and bubble lights up top. We reach it in another second. Without saying much else he grabs a light pack, lighter than mine, and points to the trailhead. In his hand, he's holding an evidence bag with a piece of clothing—a pink, studded blouse.

I take it, unzip the bag and bring the pink material to Shady's snout. She sits and studies it, sniffing it. I look at her, especially her eyes, and this time she's surprising me. Usually she attacks her marker. For some reason she's approaching this one with a care I'm not used to. It's almost like she's reading it, seeing in it something the rest of us can't appreciate.

When I'm satisfied she's got the scent, I hand the blouse back to Murphy. After putting that away, his hand comes out of his pack holding a Spiderman T-shirt. It's small, I note, as he takes it out of its evidence bag.

"How young's the boy?" I ask.

"Seven."

I nod at that, look up at the mountains wondering which one's holding him and his sister right now.

"Shouldn't she smell his shirt, too?" Murphy asks.

"Best not. But bring it along just in case."

I keep looking at the mountains. Even in

August they seem cold and full of jagged cruelty, like other mountains I know. For a moment I wonder how close to the mountains I'll have to get, whether I'll have to climb them. The thought knots my insides, and I fight the urge to freeze. No more of that, I tell myself.

"They've been out there now one day, right?" I ask.

"And a night."

I think on that. They didn't call me straight away, thinking they could handle it on their own. That means more time out there for those kids, a colder trail for us, and fainter scents for Shady.

"Let's get, then," I say as Shady and I aim for the trailhead.

Murphy catches up to us as we traverse the first, gradual rise. I gesture to him to walk behind us, and he gets it without instruction. Without explanation from him I guess he's been in several of these chases, enough to know not to step in front of the dog.

We go a ways before he breaks the silence

with, "Before we get too far into this, I just wanted to say what..." For the third time, his throat needs clearing.

He stammers the way people do when they want to say something nice and respectful, but their pride or their fear or their shyness, or all of those things combined prevents them from saying what they should, from treating people like they ought to be treated. I've seen it before. In hospitals. In airports. At the grocery store. At the start of a Fourth of July parade. The good ones go to say it, and something catches in their throat. The hypocrites spout something stupid. The ones that would rather not think about it too hard smile at you maybe, then look away as if life is nothing but having nice jobs and tall houses and big cars and wafer-thin cellphones that they use to be social with people who they don't give a flip about.

"I wanted to say what an honor it is to serve with you," Murphy says. To his credit, he leaves it there. Simple, straight-up, none of the syrup, all that needs stating, with the unsaid part still ringing loud and clear.

Even so, I have to fight off the urge of replying with my cynical acid. "Thanks," I say. "Hope I can help today."

"If not today, then maybe tomorrow," he says. "We got you for two days, right?"

"Yeah. Normally I'd linger longer if needed, but I got some business to tend to. Clear down all the way to Texas, so lots of driving."

"Oh? What's down there?"

"An Army base," I say. "Lackland. My home base, actually."

"You still go down there?"

I could tell him I do, once every six weeks, to check in with my VA shrink, even though I see a local shrink more regularly. I could also tell him I go down there to kibitz with my current CO, all part of a special arrangement I shouldn't discuss outside official venues.

I opt for saying, "Don't go down there often. Only as part of my reserve duty. But this is a special occasion. A buddy of mine's coming home. Wanna be there to give him a proper welcome."

Murphy starts going on about how great it is to be there when vets come home. He's asking about whether this is my buddy's last tour. Something catches in my throat when I go tell him it is, and not by his choice or per the Army's plan. But Shady interrupts us with a lunge forward, straining for a small bridge crossing over a creek.

At this point I would pull back and scold her, but I'm glad to trot after her and run away from the conversation.

The wood moans as we cross the bridge. Behind us Murphy's asking whether Shady's onto something. I'm thinking no, probably some critter's got her attention. But then she stops. Just beyond the bridge she sniffs the air to her right, like she senses something in the bit of tan dirt that scurries under a thick bush to join the creek down below.

I look to my left, up trail, where a bunch of footprints and a couple of paw print patterns tell me which way the search party went.

"How many other dogs?" I ask.

"Two," Murphy replies.

Not best, and I know a day after the fact, between wind and crews contaminating the scene, I ain't got much of a hope. Well, not with Shady. Unless...

I nod. "OK."

"She think they went down there?"

"Yeah, maybe." I hesitate. Shady hasn't proven trustworthy, not one hundred percent, and though I wouldn't doubt a more reliable animal, I do now.

"Might make sense," Murphy says. "Just the thing kids might do, go down to the creek to play."

"Might be." I lean down, cursing again my inability to crouch by my dog, the way I would like to. The way I used to.

Still, I bend down low enough to look into Shady's eyes. She glances up at me for a moment before she returns her full attention to the bush and the patch of dirt under it.

"The parents said the kids normally went up

this trail a bit," Murphy says. "They would stay on the flat part, then turn around before it started climbing. Always on trail. That's where the search party's been concentrating. There's no trail down there, I guess is what I'm trying to say."

When I don't comment, he comes back with. "Is she a tracker or an air scent dog?"

Great, so he's Googled himself an education on the difference between tracking and air scent dogs. He's probably figured that since I had her take in the girl's scent from an item of clothing, she's a tracker. But he's also probably picked up that Shady hasn't done the whole job nose down to the ground. She's sniffing the air, too, like an air scent dog would. Well, I guess I should give him credit for paying attention.

I don't want to get into a discussion, so I just say, "She's mostly tracking right now. But she can do both."

"I thought they had to be trained to—"

I raise my hand to signal a stop. Shady's still sniffing at the air between her and the bush. Is she tracking? Is she sniffing the air? Who cares? We're on the job here. And Shady's actually managing to stay on her best game so far.

"Good girl," I whisper. I weigh my choices for another moment before I unleash her and give her the command to go. *"Revier."*

To my surprise, she doesn't jump out, but instead slinks her way under the bush and steps down the steep incline like a cat stalking prey. I hear her heavy snorts, taking whatever scent she's grabbed onto for all she's got. When I lose sight of her, I stomp back onto the bridge to watch her from there. I see her come out of the bushes, nose down, sniffing out the pebbled creek shore. She keeps that up for a minute or so, then hops forward, stops, does it some more.

That's when it happens. She stands still, head raised and ears pointing straight up, nose sniffing at the mountains. She stays like that for a few moments and lurches forward into a full sprint.

"Steh Auf," I shout.

She stops and turns her head toward me. The

way she looks at me, I know what's coming next.

"*Steh Auf*," I scream, letting my voice go shrill.

She takes off nonetheless, faster this time.

I try another command. "*Bliff.*" It's no use. She's gone.

"Dutch commands, right?" Murphy is saying as I rush past him. "Search and stand, right?"

"We have to get down there," I tell him.

I stop to glance at him, and he's looking at me. No doubt unable to help himself, his eyes scan my legs.

"Worry about not breaking your own neck, big boy," I tell him. "I can handle myself."

Chapter 2

It takes us ten minutes to find an alternative, more gradual way down to the creek, and another twenty minutes to catch up with Shady. By then, walking as best we can along the meandering creek, we've reached the base of the hills. Shady is standing there, at attention, head and nose pointed toward the mountains.

"You really think they came this way?" Murphy asks. "I can see them going down to the creek back there, but considering how hard it's been on us, I doubt they'd want to make a go of it this far up."

I bend down to pet Shady. I could scold her for bolting on me, but right now I'm thinking we have more important things to consider.

Besides, she did finally stand, on her own terms, sure, but here she is, standing.

Shady whimpers.

"What's wrong girl?" I ask her.

She lets out another whimper, a longer one she exhales like a sharp whistle.

I straighten out and look up at the mountains in the distance. Up closer, I see the creek start to climb up. Around it, I don't see much by the way of trails we or anyone else could use to get up there, to those sheer cliffs. Yet here we are, next to a dog with a nose pointing in that direction.

"You didn't answer my question," Murphy says, a hint of annoyed impatience coloring his voice.

"What's that?"

"The kids wouldn't come this far. Even if they did, at this point they would turn around wouldn't they?"

I am scanning our surroundings for evidence of their passing when I see it. From my backpack I detach one of my telescoping walking sticks. I expand it and use it to point at a spot by the water.

"Here," I tell him. "A footprint."

"That's not a kid's shoe," he points out.

"That it aint." I look around some more.

This pebbled surface isn't much for capturing footprints, except by the water where it's muddy. I tell myself this is why I haven't noticed anything up to now, but truth is, my one fourth American Indian tracker lineage notwithstanding, I've come to over-rely on my dog. Lately I've tried to up my game, but I still ain't much of anything without a dog. Lucky me I have Shady.

Still, after thinking about it for a bit, I notice it. "Here," I tell Murphy. "Not an outline of a print, because of the pebbles, but if you look at the ones that dig deeper into the dirt, you can estimate the size of a footprint. The more they dig in, the heavier the foot, too."

Murphy nods. He catches on quick enough to say, "I'm noticing a couple of big ones over here."

"Any small ones?" I ask, already knowing the answer for myself.

"Yeah, two sizes, I think."

"More or less what I'm seeing on my end." I look up at him to see his expression, his lips parted in mid breath. "I know I'm not law enforcement, and it's not my place to say, but we ain't just looking for two little ones."

He takes that in for a moment and comes back at me with, "Yeah, well, three sets of footprints is one thing. But we don't know they were set at the same time."

"That's an argument for a defense lawyer to make in a court of law. This ain't no court of law. This is the great outdoors, and our job is to track what we see. Right now I'm seeing three, not two."

He stares at me for a second before he pulls out his radio. "Murphy here," he says. "We went up the creek."

"You did what?"

"That's where my tracker took me."

They start hassling him about going off-trail,

then crack him a couple of clever ones about being up a creek without a paddle. They have the good sense to exclude any comments about being there with a cripple passing herself for a world class tracker.

I turn my back to him and join Shady. Like her I look up the creek and sniff the air between us and the nearby cliffs. We gotta go up there, she's thinking, and even while I'm not looking forward to it, I agree.

They're up there.

I close my eyes and feel a cool breeze wafting in from that hard rock. Though I try not to go there, I find myself half a world away, feeling a cold wind coming from more brutal mountain ranges. I want to hear the squawking of the radio and the blabbering between Murphy and whoever's on the other side of his radio link. Instead, I only hear the bleating of goats and the strange words of Afghan shepherds. They're up there, the missing, the wounded. I and my Shadow have to go find them.

"McMurtry," I hear my CO say, but it's not

him. It's Murphy, here, trying to get my attention.

"Call me Jane," I tell him. "McMurtry's too much of a mouthful."

He smiles at that, barely. "The Chief and a deputy are headed our way. The rest of them will keep searching where they are."

I nod, restraining the urge to say that's fine by me, that the we don't need the whole posse trampling my track.

"They want us to wait until they get here."

"That doesn't sound terribly clever," I reply.

I remove my backpack to release my other walking stick. I unfurl it, re-strap my backpack, and I click both sticks together. This is my little deflection. I smile at Murphy to conceal how I hate using them. They look cool, like beefed up skiing poles. Still, they are what they are, primarily, my admission—which I've put off up to this point as we clambered up the creek—that I can't bank on a steady balance. I've told myself plenty it ain't no such thing, that anyone trekking through rough country should use these. But the self-reproach of an amputee's mind doesn't surrender with ease.

"We really should wait here," Murphy says. "If you're right about the larger prints—"

"What? We need reinforcements?" I point at Shady. "She doesn't just track, if you get my meaning."

"But the chief—"

"The chief fills out your performance review, not mine. You can sit here if you'd like. I'm pushing ahead."

He rubs his neck. "I'm not privy to all the details of your contract. But I thought you were always supposed to defer to local law enforcement direction."

"I get the chain of command thing. But that last job I did, not far from here in Louisville? We near lost the track of those kids from all our sitting around to wait for this person to arrive or that other thing to happen."

I leave it there, knowing I don't have to reiterate any of the details. With all the TV coverage I got on that job, he should remember how the missing kids spent a night and two days away from their parents because we couldn't get to tracking early enough, when we only had to go in two miles to get to them. Though I came out smelling like a rose out of that one, savior coronation and all, I secretly kicked myself for not being more forceful. Ain't going to let that regret smack me again, and I stare Murphy down to let him know so.

He shakes his head, looking around at the bushes and the stream like he is going to find an answer there. I hear my mom's voice again, counseling me to treat boys nice.

"Look," I add. "Light's getting short. It's what now, 3 PM? We cool our heels here another thirty to forty minutes, and by the time your folks join the fun, it's near time to pack it in."

I say that knowing that in all likelihood I won't go down to camp when evening comes. At least me and Shady will be spending the night on one of them cliffs. I eye Murphy's flimsy backpack and his cute shorts, and I know he didn't plan for that. At some point he'll be wanting to head back to camp.

But they're up there, my newest buddies. And I ain't letting go of the scent this time. I aim to get them down these cliffs tonight, or the night after, if that's what it takes.

Murphy vacillates some more. I don't give him a chance to conjure any further objections.

"*Sook*," I tell Shady. "Slow," I add, and this time she heeds me, walking off more or less a few steps in front of me, nose up creek.

Up to now, I've contemplated the concern that along this creek, it would be far too easy to lose the scent. All anyone has to do is walk in the water, and the scent has nothing to latch onto. Maybe this won't turn as negative as a set of adult prints might suggest. Whoever we're tracking isn't trying to lose us. Or maybe, my more cynical side rebuts, they don't know enough to evade us. Maybe some creep followed these two kids and then...

I shake that off. It's not my place. Sure, I've been reading some police investigation manuals so I can have more of a clue as I go around the country to offer my services. But I don't know jack, and I ain't going to play detective here. I'm the tracker. Best focus on one thing and do it well, a voice from my past tells me. As I start up the steep side of the creek, that's what I aim to do.

If you've ever hiked in the high country and disobeyed the advice to never go off-trail, you know making your own way where there ain't none is tough. Seeing where to go without the benefit of someone having drawn you some nice switchbacks that make easier work of a climb doesn't come without struggle. You will also know that if you have an eye for it, you can find where the animals go. Deer in particular make their own trails, usually along water sources, in and out of them.

I look for that now. As I climb, watching Shady struggle with how to make her way, I soon realize following the creek won't work for long. We turn around a bend in the rock, and confirmation comes when we see fingers of water flowing from up above, down the rock face, to feed the head of the creek at the foot of the cliffs.

"*Hierr*," I say to Shady, asking her to come back to me.

She stops, in her own way realizing that she has nowhere to go. She sniffs the air, turns to me, sniffs it some more.

"*Hierr*," I repeat.

She looks up at me and comes back toward me. When she reaches me, she doesn't stop like she's supposed to.

I turn to see where she's going, nose low to the ground, and I see it: the deer trail. Murphy is standing at the head of it, oblivious to its existence, and I missed it too, so keen on looking forward and keeping eyes on Shady when I walked by it. He too watches her go past him.

"They came this way," I explain to him. "Then they turned around and went up that trail."

"I'm loving your dog," he says.

"You can keep her when this is over."

Shady stops, looks back at me and whimpers.

"*Sook,*" I tell her, followed by, "slow."

She does the tracking part, but this time not so slow.

"She's got something?" Murphy says as I go past him.

"Yeah, maybe."

The trail rises at this point, but deer know their business, and it's a gradual climb along a sheer rock face that rises to our right. Soon, though, the comfort of the forest to our left drops off. Now we're walking along a narrow trail with a long throw down to the tree line on our left and nothing to hang onto on the rock wall to our right.

"Slow," I shout after Shady, but by now she too has grown cautious, proceeding at a slower pace.

I catch up with her, before we're about to go around a bend leading to a pile of boulders. She stops. I stop behind her. Together we sniff the air.

I smell it, probably long after Shady. Not the putrid scent that forces you to cover your nose, not the sharp iron edge of spilled blood, but the oppression of it, its despair.

Death is here.

She whimpers. With a glance at me, she lets out one howling bark.

"She found something?" Murphy asks.

I whisper, "Yeah, maybe."

I step around Shady, and she follows me, whimpering as she goes. The sharp pitch of her voice drills through me. Yeah, that's it, Shady. That's how I feel all the time.

She leaps past me to climb one, then two of the boulders. There, as the western sky starts to dim, she stops. She's never done this before, but she does it now. As if to tell me she could have done this, too, up in those forsaken Afghan mountains, she cranes her neck upward and lets out one long mournful howl.

It pierces through me, and I fight back the urge to let out a howl of my own, though I think it would feel so good right about now. Not that I could. I've stopped breathing.

Murphy lets out a growl of a curse. He smells it too now, in his own way.

He steps around me to climb up the boulders.

Shady lets out another howl, shorter this time. She turns to look at Murphy as he stands atop the third layer of boulders. He looks down, then up, then back down.

He stays there, waiting for me as I navigate the easiest way up the boulders. With an outstretched arm he pulls me up the last bit of the way.

There I see her. "The girl," I say. Her body lies contorted. Little blood other than a thin, winding line seeps from her nostrils. "She fell," I add, realizing why Murphy was looking up.

"From up there, I'd guess." He points up the rock wall. "Hard slog to get up there."

"The trail must keep going beyond these boulders." To confirm my guess, I step onto another bolder to see where the trail continues, steeper now, still rising up along the rock wall. I point it out.

"Still, not easy going," he says.

"But if someone's chasing you. Or forcing you—" I stop myself there, once more telling myself I'm not here to solve or theorize about anything. With a glance at the dipping sun, I return to my tracking mindset.

"We gotta keep going," I say. "Before sunset."

"No, we have to stay here, with the body."

"You have to stay here." I take off my pack to dig out a head lamp. I put it on to show him the level of my preparedness.

"No, you have to stay here, too."

"We've been over this. I don't—."

"Look at her," he says. "Her neck in particular. What do you see?"

I let the light of my headlamp fall on her. A quick look confirms why I should stick to tracking. I see it now, and he spotted it at once.

"Her neck's bruised," I say.

"That's right. Ligature marks. She was strangled before the fall. Someone wanted to make it look like she fell. But she was dead before she hit the rocks. Only God knows for how long."

I sigh, knowing where he's going with this.

"Whoever did that is still up there," he says. "We're not going up there alone, and you sure aren't going up on your own."

He doesn't have to tell me the rest, namely that he can't go on, this now being a crime scene and all. He needs to stay with the body to safeguard the scene, and also to keep away whatever critters might come to feast on it.

"I have her," I said, pointing at Shady.

"Still, no go, Jane. That guy could be armed."

I reach into my pack and take out the heaviest item in there. "So am I. License to carry and all."

Chapter 3

Up trail Shady and I find more fingers of water tracing down the rock. Shady spots where a couple of fingers feed a round bowl-shaped slot in the rock before draining down to the forest below. She meanders around the slick rock while I implore her to be careful, in English. She makes it there to lap it up near empty. Looking at me, she waits for it to refill, then turns to drink again.

The sight of that makes me feel a little stupid for coming up here all this way, and guilty, too, for not bringing enough water for her. But I guess God provided, I say to myself as I drink from the jug I rationalized would be enough for both of us.

I wipe my mouth and try to swipe away my guilt in the same gesture. Over the next few minutes, I use my filtering kit to refill the jug from nature's water bowl. Though I reckon the water's coming straight from snow melt and touching nothing but rock on the way down, I filter it nonetheless. I have the time. No need to chance getting sick out here.

Darkness is descending on us, the last of the western light vanishing over the top of the mountains. A few steps beyond the water, I find a nook in the rock, not quite a cave, but enough to pass the night. Taking off my backpack first, I drop more than squat down onto the cold rock floor and find the best place to rest.

"*Hierr,*" I tell Shady. "Sit."

She does both, lying down next to me with another of her sorry whimpers. The sound of her voice reminds me of why she washed out of the Shadow training program. She's too much of a whiner, too noisy for her own good.

From my backpack I take out a bag with high energy pellets and I rip it open. A second later, she's lapping up the pellets into her mouth until they're all gone. Without my permission, she gets up, goes down trail, where in the quiet of the night I can hear her drinking more water. She comes back and reclaims her position next to me.

"Good girl," I say, meaning it for once as I pet her. As the last of the light disappears, I remind myself she's all I got. At least for now, anyway.

A quick pang of fear sweeps through me. I shove it away, telling it I've experienced much darker, colder places. If a murdering maniac comes for me, I have a gun and a dog, so go ahead. I'd love to put a couple in you or shred you to death, whichever comes first, or both of the above. Besides, that nut job is a coward, going after kids like that. Last thing he'll want to do is take his chances with someone who can shoot or bite back.

To show I mean it, I release my legs. I set them aside and let the cool of the rock shoot up through what's left of my knees. It is here and now I feel it, the exhaustion of the day crashing down on me, all at once. I grimace at the chaffing, too, because I forgot to put lotion on my knees before I strapped my special legs.

In what's left of the light I can see Shady look at my legs, at me, back at my legs. "Are you nuts?" I imagine her asking.

"You'll protect me, won't you girl?" I ask her.

She snorts and lays down flat.

"I'll take that as a yes." I stroke her rough coat, and I see her eyes close halfway. "You're tired, too, ain't ya? Well, now you know what it's like. After tonight you'll see what you missed. Well, you'll be able to imagine it, anyway. It's not like the be-all-that-you-can-be brochures promise."

She moans, twice, and perks her ears.

I tense up, reaching for the gun.

But then her ears drop and her eyes close almost all the way. I go back to stroking her.

"We're going to see him tomorrow. Well, actually the day after, but we'll leave tomorrow.

He can tell you the all about them cold nights we spent butt-to-butt, keeping each other warm in that pile of rubble someone calls Afghanistan."

She moans again, but this time only because she wants me to rub somewhere else. I shift my petting down, closer to her rump, and she shifts her weight as if to arrange herself in a way that will make the most of it.

I stop talking. No matter how much I love dogs and respect their intelligence, I have no misconception about them understanding anything but simple commands you drill into them over and over again. That's not to say they don't understand you. They can read you like a book, actually. They know your moods, they know you're getting sick before you even feel the first sniffle, and they sure know how to get you to do right by them if you're so inclined of heart.

None of that happens through words, though. They get to know you on a different plane, one much deeper and direct, I'd say, than words can allow. Which often makes me wonder why we humans spend so much time with words and miss the real way to connect with and care for others.

That's how it was over there. Those guys I went with on my glorious missions, they didn't talk much except to say yes sir, no ma'am, or to spout all the Special Ops lingo. But don't you think we didn't know one another. We did. Not because of what we said, but because of what we did, and what we were to each other.

That's the way it was with Shadow, too. Especially with him.

Maybe I'll tell my shrink that when I meet her next. Enough with the words already. And here's why. Just look at the way dogs do it. That'll go over well.

I am thinking all this, and I'm beginning to regret having pushed ahead, forced the issue so I could—what?—spend an adventuresome night up here on this jagged cliff? The regret doesn't come from fear. Again, I'm all done with that. In fact, in some ways, maybe I'm here because I want someone to put an end to me. No, I'm regretting it because I knew it would put me back in Afghanistan, bringing back all those cold, tense nights, and I came here anyway.

What for? For my own version of prolonged exposure therapy? Yeah, that'll go really well, too, when I tell my therapist about it.

But if I push up tomorrow morning at first light, if Shady and I track down that boy and get him back to his parents, that'll be worth it, won't it? Sure it will. Sure. Sure. I say that over and over again, and still I find no conviction in it.

The last of the light ebbs away, and darkness takes over in full.

Besides me, Shady is snoring softly. She's got the right idea. I close my eyes and rest my head against the rock face. Its coolness trickles through my hair.

The coolness tingles through me and carries me to a different mountain. I am sitting there with Shadow. The commandos he and I led here as we tracked the scent of a missing soldier have gone ahead, up trail. It is too dangerous for the girl to push ahead with them. So they've left her here with her dog, a rifle and a crack in the rock for her to hide. The mountain feels cold to the touch. Though I try to shield myself from it, its frozen fingers hold me in their grasp.

Shadow draws near, sharing some of his warmth, standing in front of me to block the worst of the cold. He takes it in his chest, he stares it down, that wind that shoots across the canyon from the taller, snow-capped mountains to the north.

I drape my arms around him and pull him back toward me, but he growls. He aims his snout at the trail below, and through my arm I feel his throat rumble.

"What is it, boy?" I whisper.

He lets out a short snort, letting out one warm, precious breath that shoots up into the night sky. His ears point up. In another moment I hear it, too, the crunch of gravelly rock underfoot. Too noisy, I tell myself, for the thin, light footwear of our enemies. But what if they're wearing boots? Some of them do, though soon I feel my body relax when I see them through my night vision goggles.

"Our boys," I tell Shadow. "All's good," I add, and he too relaxes.

I'm beginning to drift to sleep when Shady sits up. She lets out a low growl.

With the gun in my hand, I consider whether to go for my head lamp, turn it on. No, it'll give my position away. Too bad I don't have night vision goggles for this op.

Shady is pointing down trail, though, and I relax a bit. I reckon our alleged bad guy is up trail, far above me on the next ridge up, actually, if he hasn't moved on from there yet after shoving that girl over the edge. Still, I can't be sure. Maybe he's been hiding somewhere along the trail all along. Then again, a bear or a mountain lion could be heading my way, too.

Shady whimpers now. I grasp my handgun.

"Who is it, girl?" I ask her.

She makes to go down trail to meet whatever or whoever is coming up.

I hold on to her collar. *"Bliff,"* I say, giving her the stay command.

Her neck relaxes, and she sits back on her haunches.

Now I see it, a bouncing small light coming around the bend in the trail. Shady welcomes that with a bark that shouldn't but startles me nonetheless. I point the gun down trail.

"McMurtry? Jane?" I hear Murphy yelling out.

"Jesus, man," I shout back. "What the hell are you doing? You almost got a mouthful of teeth and a couple of bullets."

"Nah, Shady wouldn't do that," he says lowering his voice as he approaches. "You on the other hand, I can't be too sure."

I have to laugh at that, if nothing else because it unwinds me.

"I thought you had a crime scene to guard."

"That's taken care of." He squats and takes off his backpack.

I notice it seems heavier now, the way it hits the ground. He's also wearing full length pants, and I realize his shorts were the zip-up kind. Maybe he was more ready than I gave him credit for. I go to ask him whether his buddies brought him some supplies, but I notice him looking at my legs. My stumps, that is.

He looks away when he catches on I've spotted him. "Anyway, glad to find you. Glad you didn't go too far up trail, too." He clicks off the lamp and darkness wraps all around us again.

We say nothing to each other for what must be two or three minutes.

I hear him take a long breath before he breaks the silence with, "You know, there's no shame in it. Not one bit."

"I know that."

He takes another breath. "Know this, too. You're a damn hero. All the way through, up and down, left and right. No shame, no pity, all pride. That's all I see here."

I let his words drift in the dark. They feel

good, just right and warm. I let them linger, bask in them, even if only a little, because I don't feel worthy of them.

"You served, Dan?" I ask, realizing I've switched to his first name.

"Nah. Tried out for the team." He lets out half-hearted chuckle. "Didn't pass the physicals."

"That's too bad. Maybe you could've been a bang-up hero, too."

He takes yet another breath. "I know you did that for me. For us."

"Sure, for God and country. Do you really believe that, Dan? That we do it for you?"

"Yeah." The way he says that almost sounds like a question. "Why do you think you did it?"

"Truth is, Dan, I have no idea. We do a lot of things, send a lot of young ones out into the world, give ourselves nifty speeches to make us feel better about doing it. But God only knows what the real meaning or goal of it is."

I halt there, seeing what he says to that. At this point most people would come back with something. To his credit, he keeps listening.

"I'll tell you this, though. When you're getting shot out there, in the middle of nowhere, when you're feeling blood and flesh from your buddies splattering on you, the last thing you're thinking is what cause or mission you're there to fulfill."

I pause again. This time I want him to say something, but he doesn't.

"Ever been in a shoot-out, Dan?"

"Can't say that I have."

"It would be like that. You signed up to protect and to serve. That might be what got you there, but when things blow up around you, you're thinking of two things: how do I get myself out of here, and how do I get my buddies to go with me. The good ones think mostly on the second."

"And I'm sure that was you, thinking on the second."

"That's awful sure of you. How do you figure?"

"Why are you here, charging up this

mountain, sleeping on some rock? Because you're thinking of getting yourself out of here?"

His question cuts into me like jagged shrapnel. Did he, while jabbering on his radio, somehow notice the way I was looking up at the mountain? Did he put that together with another day, not that long ago, when I wanted to charge up a mountain to chase down someone in trouble? Now I'm really doing some crazy talk. No way he's put all that together, but maybe he senses it in a different way.

"I don't know, Dan. I guess I don't know that either."

"Sure you do."

"Yeah, maybe."

"You say that a lot," he says. "Yeah, maybe."

"It's my positive outlook. Yeah for the positive part, maybe for admitting in life nothing's for sure."

He chuckles at that. In the dark, it sounds forced. "You need some rest. I'll take first watch," he suggests.

"With Shady here, no one else takes first or

second watch," I tell him. "That's why the boys loved having me along. You probably need some rest too. Take it."

I close my eyes and listen for his breath, waiting for confirmation that he's fallen asleep. I never get it. My eyes grow heavy, and I let myself sink into the hard, cold rock.

Chapter 4

To my shame, I wake up last. Shady is sitting next to Dan as he works a small cylindrical contraption. A small portable stove, I realize once my eyes clear.

"Hope you like oatmeal," he says.

"Don't love it, don't hate it."

"Shady seems pretty interested."

"And she'll seem pretty sick if you give it to her."

"I thought oats were good for dogs."

"This one's special."

"I can see that." He takes a second, as if weighing what he says next. "Doesn't seem to mind too well for a highly trained dog."

"Hmm. Let's just say she's got a creative,

more open-minded approach. She does well in the end, I suppose."

"She does pretty well by you."

"Is that what them web blogs say about me?"

He smiles. "Yeah, maybe."

I smile back. "What's our plan?"

"I would tell you, but I'm sure you can do one better."

I wink at him now. "You catch on quick. Must be that Irish working for ya."

He returns his attention to the stove, swirls a small wooden spoon around, then looks up at me.

"I meant what I said last night," he says.

"Careful now, Dan. Don't go getting too sweet on me. My bite's worse than hers."

"Enough said, then."

"Yeah, maybe."

We laugh together. A warmth rises in my face, and I rush to conceal it. I can't remember the last time I flirted with a boy, and here I am on the edge of it, maybe a little farther than that. I look away and catch sight of my legs. That's how I pull away, or so I tell myself as I busy myself with putting them back on. This time I remember to get the gel out of my backpack's front pocket to rub over my knees before I strap on the prosthetics.

The thought persists, though, and I ask myself again about the last time I tried my luck with a guy. It's been a long time, for sure, before I signed on, when Dad was still alive to take a goofy snapshot of me and some guy before we ran off to a church social.

I guess Dan isn't bad looking, nice enough, big strapping guy who knows his way around the great outdoors, if his skill with a portable camping stove gives accurate indication. But then I remember me, how I've looked pretty much since my sophomore year in high school: big, lumbering, menacing and intimidating, like one girl told me using her big words. As I strap on my second leg I run headlong into the other reason I should stop this flirting nonsense.

I'm damaged goods.

When I'm done, I consider the best way to go

over to Dan and Shady. I could just slide over on my butt, but I don't want to. Standing up, using one or two of my walking sticks will be no problem either, if a little awkward and only a hair less embarrassing than the butt sliding approach.

I'm still weighing my options when I see Dan stand up and come over to me with an outstretched hand. I normally wouldn't take it. Truly, folks, I don't need it, and I despise the way people think they have to help me. I'm fine, really. Stop opening doors for me when you open them for no one else. Stop giving me your seats. Stop suggesting the elevator. Above all, enough with the furtive looks and the useless pity.

All that said, I look into his eyes, and I know I need to take his hand.

He pulls me up, all one hundred and sixty pounds of me, like I'm a ten pound gym dumbbell.

"Thanks."

"Don't mention it."

"Thanks for coming last night, too," I tell him.

"When you get down this hill, you'll have a mom and a dad who will thank you for finding their little girl."

"Will I?"

He thinks about that. "If they don't, someone should."

"Yeah, maybe."

He shakes his head and lets out a hardy laugh. "You're a little friendlier *and* funnier when you get some sleep."

"Always been a morning person, I guess."

"Good. Let's shove this grub down before your gal there takes it all, and then let's get this thing done."

We eat fast, pack up everything, and head out. Once more, Shady leads the way, tail wagging as she goes. An hour into it, around 8 AM, Dan's radio beeps.

"Murphy here."

"You guys on the move?"

"Yup, up trail as of an hour ago."

"OK, keep going. You're going to get some help up top."

That's when I hear it, the familiar sound rising up from the valley floor. "Helo," I mutter.

"What?" Murphy asks me.

"Helicopter." I point it out in the sky. Sandy barks at it for punctuation.

On the radio, his boss is saying, "Feds. For some reason, they want to join the search."

"Tell them to stay aloft," I say to Dan. "They can help us spot from above, we do the flushing down below."

He repeats that into the radio. That's how it should work. That's how we used to do it. But something tells me my suggestion will go unheeded.

"Negative. They're bringing in some personnel," the Chief replies.

"That's crazy. There's nowhere to land up there," Dan shouts into the radio to counter the rising sound of the approaching aircraft.

"It's a drop," I say. "They're dropping them in."

Shady is barking now, almost non-stop. She's furious. For once we're one hundred percent of the same mind. I'm wishing I could snarl and bark and bare my teeth too right now. I start marching up the trail, figuring I'll do that up top, up close and personal.

Dan gets off the radio and shouts after me. I can't hear him inside the helicopter's engine rumble. Shady races past me, and I speed up to keep up with her. They're going to screw this whole thing up. These clueless bastards are going to spook the target, have already spooked the target, actually, unless he or they are heavily medicated or inebriated, and I can't do a thing about it except race up and hope somehow I can beat them.

I'm running, these magical legs giving me enough spring to make my step almost light. Or maybe it's the fury inside me, that same fury that boiled when they stopped me last time, when all anybody wanted to do was get there and find bodies we could put in neat caskets, draped in brand new flags, to stuff them into a cargo plane on their way back for hollow honor and meaningless pomp.

Dan catches up with me, asks me, "What's going on?"

"Stupidity, from the looks of it." I glance over at him and add, "Get that boy's shirt ready. We're going to need it."

The helicopter hovers over us and floats above the ridge. We're almost there, almost, but we won't beat them. I look up and see a tether swinging down, one uniformed figure hanging from it, another at the ready to winch down.

My thighs are burning. I won't stop, though. It may look ugly, it may look awkward, but I'm making it up to that ridge, and then Shady and I are going to track that boy.

"The shirt!" I yell.

Dan keeps pace next to me, slings his backpack off one shoulder, holding it with the other. The shirt comes out of the front pocket. Good for him, planning ahead by keeping it within easy reach.

"Shady, *Hierr!*"

Shady stops, looks back at me, then bounds down trail toward us with the same urgency I feel. When she reaches us I shove the shirt into her snout. She sniffs it with the fury of a shark swimming in blood. I let her go on for a few seconds before I shout the seek command.

"Revier!"

She takes off up trail like a missile honing in on its target. That's when I acknowledge her challenge. Once she reaches the top, the wind that helicopter's blades are blowing down will cast away any floating scents, and confuse any that may have latched onto surfaces or vegetation.

I stop and I wave up at the helicopter. "Get off! Get away!"

But they can't hear me, won't hear me, won't care if they do hear me, won't mind ruining everything as they drop one, two, three, four, five commandos.

"What the hell is going on?" Dan asks. "Why do we need paramilitary here?"

We reach the top. I search for Shady. I see

her, running in circles. From time to time she stops, barking up at the helicopter, her own way of telling them to move the hell away so she can do her job.

The commandos are walking toward us. To Dan's visible relief, though they have small machine guns, they're keeping them at their side. They approach us with hands up, the universal just-stay-calm-and-no-one-gets-hurt sign.

I start running toward them, and Dan follows. Five steps into my sprint, my foot catches on something, and I stumble. Dan catches me before I fall all the way, holds me up. I elbow him away and start running again. When I get to the first guy, I barrel into him and take him down clean off his feet.

Dan is on me in a few seconds. He lifts me up by my belt, and I feel like that lightweight dumbbell again.

"Alright, everybody stay cool!" Dan is shouting. He's got his hands out to the two closest uniformed idiots who are actually pointing their side arms at us.

"What the hell do you clowns think you're doing?" I scream at the top of my lungs. "We got a scent here, and you come and you kick it all over the Rockies with your damn helicopter! A little boy is going to die, never see the light of day because of you! Are you proud? Are you serving your country now? Just let me know where to pin your medal!"

"Ma'am, please, let's settle down," the guy I tackled says, now propped up on one knee, like he's begging me, maybe next up he'll whip out the wedding ring. He's just a kid, farm boy from somewhere by the looks of him, should be modeling overalls and tractors. God, what has happened to me, to us?

Something pops inside me and my fury deflates into leaden despair. It feels like one of those boulders where I stood looking down at a dead girl, except now it's on top of me, pounding me into the earth.

I feel like I'm falling when I see Shady racing toward us, snarling, teeth showing in all her anger. The men turn their guns toward her, and I stumble toward her.

"No! Don't you dare shoot her!" I call out to her too, in every command I can remember and a few I make up. Her eyes are not on me. They're focused on them, the danger, and I keep stumbling toward her until somehow I fall on her and hang on, wrestling her to a draw to hold her in place.

"It's OK, Shady. It's OK," I whisper in her ear. "It's all over. You're safe. I'm safe." I hold her as she whimpers and barks. *"Af. Bravy. Af. Bravy,"* I add for good measure.

As I did a minute prior, Shady deflates too. I hold her, and she whimpers. I don't know which of us goes first, her or me, but we start trembling. I cry, and she whimpers some more.

Above the helicopter pulls away to hover farther off. I can hear Dan and one of the men arguing.

"We have orders to evacuate her," one of the men is saying.

"What the hell does that mean? She doesn't

need evacuating."

"She can't be here."

"What do you mean she can't be here? She's a citizen, assisting with a search and rescue operation and a murder investigation, by the way. Helped us find a dead girl's body last night, and she was this close from finding her little boy brother."

"That may be, sir, but we have orders to take her back to base."

"Why?"

"We don't have that information."

"Like hell you don't," Dan says.

"What he means," I cut in. "Is that he can't tell you the information." I look up at the guy Dan's arguing with, same kid I tackled. "I need to talk to your CO. Your commanding officer, in case they went up and changed the acronym since I was in."

"Yes, ma'am. Can do. He's your CO, too."

I stand up. "Then I rather talk to him one on one."

"Will do, Major."

I almost tell him to call me by my proper rank, Captain, not the thing they stuck into me while lying on a hospital bed because they felt sorry for me. But he's just a kid, a cog in the machine. This is none of his fault. He's just following orders.

"What's going on, Jane?" Dan asks me.

"Hang on to your hat, Dan," I tell him. "You're about to witness something cool. You're about to see how real damn heroes go out when the battle's done. Or when their higher uppers say it's done, which ain't always one and the same."

I look back at the kid. "Set it up."

He radios the helicopter, and it approaches.

No more than a minute later, I'm strapped to my own harness, holding Shady under her belly and against my chest. Up I go, and for as long as I can, through vision blurred by hot tears, I stare at Dan. This is it, big boy, how heroes and their dogs go up into the sky, hopefully, to fight another day.

Chapter 5

"It wasn't my call," Lieutenant Colonel Brady tells me. He's twirling a cigar a shade lighter than his skin in his fingers. In the dim light of his office, it's hard to tell which is which.

"But you made the call," I tell him.

"It couldn't be risked."

"I love them passive sentences, especially the ones we write here in this Army. They convey little information and assign even less responsibility."

"You know what I'm talking about," he says in his best fatherly baritone intonation.

"No, actually I don't. You're going to have to draw me a real pretty picture. Sir."

He sets the cigar down. Until now he's been

sitting sideways to me, so he swivels in his chair and comes toward me, both elbows on that mahogany desk I'm sure he's so proud of.

"You know you're going to kill my career, don't you?" he says. "I'm never going to make full bird. Not if you have anything to say about it."

"Last time I checked, I have no say at all. Now, about them pretty pictures I asked for?"

"You're a public figure now, Jane. You know that." He drums his fingers on the table. "Really popular. Or, like you'd say in spite of that English major of yours, *real popular*. Instant celeb, with your heroic past and beautiful dog and an Olympic future. That there is real cashable prestige."

I have to reward him with a grin. Once more he's nailed my manner of speaking to a T. I wish we were doing it over beers rather than in here, after what's happened, before what's coming. But so is life. A little bit of "yeah," and a lot of "maybe."

"OK, so I'm a public figure. What does that

have to do with busting up a civilian search and rescue?"

"We heard you spent the night out there," he says. "That was too close to the line for some."

He leaves it there, his bit of kindness toward me. I get it. Someone pointed out my latest escapade looked too much like a prior mission— *the* mission, actually—and they hit the panic button when they thought I might flip out. Is that all, I wonder? Is there more to it? I can't figure why Army Special Ops would want to sabotage a search and rescue for a missing kid, so I have to say, yeah, that's it, even if a nagging unease remains at the back of my neck telling me there's got to be more to this.

"Shadow still getting here on time?" I ask, opting to shift subjects.

"On the dot, per the manifest."

I bite my lower lip, and I can see he's picking up on that.

"You're going to be OK?"

"Depends on how OK he is. You guys have never thought to tell me the extent of his injuries. On account of my fragile mental state, no doubt."

"They've done a lot for him. Saved his hind leg, left him with just a limp. He's moving pretty good, I hear." He pauses as if to consider how best to offer a promise he can't guarantee. "Might even shake off that limp."

"And?"

"His tracking days are over." He rattles that off as if wanting to get it out there and quick, like ripping off a bandage and all the scabs that go with it.

"I figured as much. All I want for him is to run in my ranch and chase squirrels until he's good and old."

"He should be able to do that. With limitations."

"From the sound of that, I'm guessing there's more limitations than a gimpy leg."

He leans back in his chair, and it swivels to the side with a long, piercing screech. Now it's him biting his lower lip. He picks up the cigar again, twirls it again.

"He lost one eye in the blast," Brady says. "The other one they saved, but barely. His vision is compromised."

The news shakes me as much as his face tells me he feared. But I rationalize it away. Dogs have very keen sense of hearing and smell. With training and care, he'll be able to make up for his lack of vision. Besides, he's not totally blind, and I've heard of blind dogs doing some amazing stuff. Heck, his sense of smell might intensify to make up the difference. He might even become a better tracker. And if not, he'll still be in my ranch, which in the hottest or coldest day stands way ahead of that pile of rubble he's been scratching his paws on for the past year, and the two years before that, when I was there with him.

"He'll be fine," I say.

"What about you?"

"What about me?"

"Will you be fine?"

"Finer now that he's finally with me. He should have come home with me. You know that."

"Yeah. I do."

"But that wasn't your call either."

He waves the cigar. "Been over that. Regulations."

"Right," I say, reliving how when I came home minus two lower legs, Shadow had to stay behind, like any other soldier in my detail. Never mind I was the only trainer and handler he'd ever had. Never mind taking him away from me ripped me up as much as losing my legs. Never mind him being with me would have helped me face my demons. Nah, a shrink can help you with that, your dog stays behind, and if you're lucky, you get him back blind and with a busted leg.

"I've arranged for sleeping quarters for you," he says. "You can use them, or you can drive to some flea infested motel. Got some of those nearby enough, though you will still have to drive some."

"I'd go for the fleas, but you left my 4Runner back in Boulder, remember?"

"True," he says with a smile. "My bad." He runs the cigar under his nose and adds, "Your 4Runner's on its way. Should be here midday tomorrow."

"Nice."

"You know the drill for meals and such."

"Of course."

He turns to me, takes the same I'm-about-to-tell-you-something-serious elbows on the table position he took before. "I'd like you to go by the pen."

By that he means the dog training school on base. I shrug. "Sure. Can Shady come along?"

"You know how we love alumni. They start up at 0900 sharp."

"Hmm. Getting a little lax. When I ran that shop, we got going at 0800, some days sharper than others."

He smiles. "Yeah. Those were the good old days."

"Oh, oh. Here we don't go again, do we?"

"I'd like you to think about it. For reals this time. As far as I'm concerned, no one knows K-

9s like you. You have a real talent. You feel
them. Everyone said that. It wasn't just book
knowledge and training. You understood each
one like your own. We're missing that."

"I bet you are."

"You know we invested a lot of capital in
you." He waves an index finger in my direction.
"Of the political kind, no less. Got you to do the
job only enlisted do, and we proved our point,
didn't we? Officers do bring fresh perspective
and insight to K9 training and handling." He
leaves the rest unsaid, namely the part about
women not being allowed in Special Ops, and
how he also greased the skids on that front to
get me a ride-along pass. Even if I can't put
Special Ops on my resume.

"I'm just reserves now," I say.

"That means jack to me. And I know
someone up top who feels the same way. I'll
bring you back all the way if you'll have it."

"I like my life now."

"Do you?"

"Sure. Who wouldn't? 20K followers on

Twitter. Haven't you heard?"

"Yeah, I've heard." He leans back in his chair, and it makes that same screech again. "Think it over, Jane. Serious, this time. We all need purpose."

"You mean we all need someone else to tell us our purpose."

"I ain't shoving this down your throat. Just think it over."

"Right, serious this time. Got it."

"You know… If I didn't like you like I do—" He stops, and through that hard ebony veneer I see something I haven't experienced since Dad died. "You know I see you like you're my own flesh and blood. You should. Or why else would I put up with that mouth of yours?"

I search for something clever and acid-laced to lob back, but instead I find myself enjoying the moment, longing for it to go on before he goes back to his impenetrable, all country, a little God, and nothing else self.

The next morning, after breakfast and before I head over to the K-9 pen, I call Dan on my cellphone. "How's the search going?" I ask him.

"Nothing much to report," he replies. "They took those other two dogs up top. But so far nothing. They seem pretty lost."

"Sorry to hear that."

"How are you? Everything OK?"

"I had some Army grub for dinner and breakfast this morning, but so far it doesn't look like it's going to be terminal."

He chuckles. "OK, you take care of yourself, then."

"I will." I pause before rushing to add. "You too. It was good working with you."

"Pleasure's all mine."

At that point we stop, both of us at a loss for what else to say. We stammer our way to our goodbyes and hang up.

I step out into the morning. It all comes at me with the familiarity of a home I grew up in, and the unease of a place now inhabited by strangers. If you've ever returned to a family home long sold to someone else, you know this feeling.

Here at Lackland Air Force Base in Texas, home of the Defense Military Working Dog Center, many of us will come and go, and upon coming back, we'll feel that way. We'll experience a fondness for a place that shaped us, and we'll sense we no longer belong here, not all the way, not in the way we fit and functioned before. Maybe we never fit and just didn't know it.

As I take Shady out of her overnight kennel, I ask her if she feels that, too. She doesn't tell me, of course, not with words or even with a whimper. But her keen eyes and her pricked, non-relaxing ears communicate her own flavor of inner tension all the same.

We don't go in the pen. I find a spot, far away from the dogs in training and behind a chain link fence from which Shady and I can observe.

A few of the guys inside sneak looks my way on more than one occasion. Part of me wonders if a certain Lieutenant Colonel let them know who that legendary gal standing over there is. My ego wants to believe it, anyway, but they give me little recognition and zero accolades. That's fine by me.

From a shaded spot, Shady and I watch the training. I sit on a wooden box. She rests on her haunches and keeps a watchful eye on her species. I daze through most of it, not taking particular note of any one exercise or technique. I can do all that in my sleep, and for all intents and purposes, I sleep through it now.

Toward 11:30 AM, as our shade threatens to abandon us, I hear Shady whimper. From our right, I see a tall, thick figure walking toward us. Lieutenant Colonel Brady approaches slowly, trading glances between the training arena and me.

He reaches us without a word, turns to face the pen without a word, and stands there in silence.

"I don't belong here," I say. "You know that, right?"

"I fear it."

"You don't need me here."

"You're right. But you do."

"Like I said, I don't belong here."

"And why is that, Jane?"

"My time has passed." I hear those words come out of my lips, and they ring in me the bells of sadness. How should it be that a thirty-something year old can say that? Is it true for all of my life, no matter what I try?

"We'll have to disagree on that."

"Yeah, maybe."

We stay there for a few more minutes, watching them wrap up the training session. I want to move because by now the shade is almost gone and the San Antonio sun is beating down on me hard and hot.

"I have some good news for you," Brady says.

"I need me some of those."

"I got him on an earlier flight. 1530. Figured since you're here a day earlier and he's already state-side, why not."

"Great. Thanks."

"I'll get you the runway information as soon as I have it," he says, and walks back to where he came from. Shady and I head the opposite way.

Chapter 6

As it turns out and as I figured, the runway information is irrelevant. I know the hangar area the C-17 will taxi to. I've gotten off that ride at that location plenty often. I've bounced and rattled inside that ride enough times to know what it sounds like, and I hear it before I spot it in the eastern sky. I watch that improbable flying mass grow larger, turning and gliding for home.

Strange. I feel strange again, an observer behind the chain link fence, like one having an out of body experience looking on as the landing happens to someone else.

The cargo plane lands and slows before it starts lumbering to make several turns, until it finally reaches us. The engines cut out, the back swings down, and one after the other, without much of a wait, soldiers lugging long, thick gear bags and weapon cases stream out.

Shady and I inspect each one, none of them with as much as an arm sling. I restrain the urge to resent them for that, whispering instead, "Good for you." Good that they are coming home whole, on the outside, at least, even if deeper inside they're carrying a brokenness no one on this earth can repair. Good for them whose bodies will carry them unhindered. Maybe they'll lead normal lives, with normal jobs. Maybe they'll keep that brokenness from shattering through.

"Full flight," I hear next to me, and I recognize Lieutenant Colonel Brady's voice.

"Yes, sir."

"Big welcome over at the gym," Brady adds. "Lots of anxious loved ones, streamers, posters, balloons, and screaming kids."

"You almost make me glad I never went through that," I say because from here, with my dogs on leash, I would walk over to the pen, leave them in their kennel, and go wash up in the barracks.

I start seeing that when the first handler comes out. My heart speeds up for a moment, until I realize the dog is smaller than Shadow. The next handler and dog pair don't elicit the same feeling, and neither do the next two.

I notice the fifth handler is a woman, and there I go, out of body experience again, seeing myself and not her. Only her stockier, shorter build and choppy gait break the illusion, and I think, good for her too, making it with the dogs and the boys.

"Who's she?" I ask.

"Captain select Casandra Godinez. Reminds me some of you. A little of the right kind of mentoring, and she might turn into something." He nudges me with his elbow. "I think you can guess whose mentoring I have in mind."

Godinez looks in my direction, and I think nothing of it. I think a little more when she stops at the bottom of the ramp, and turns around with her dog, a black Lab, to look up.

Shady picks it up first, and she lets out one of her sharp, howling barks, before she drops into her whimpering. At the top of the ramp, I see a big fellow, carrying a matched to his size dog, just like I carried Shady up into that helicopter. Arms under the belly, pulled up against his chest.

Godinez extends her hand toward him, as if she could catch him should he stumble. He makes it down the ramp with deliberate, sure steps. There, Godinez gestures for him to set the dog down.

"Shadow?" I whisper.

He sets him down with tenderness and care you see from few men. With his left forearm still under the dog's belly, he strokes his neck and backside. He leaves his arm there for a moment, as if to allow the dog to catch his balance. Slowly he pulls out his forearm, and the dog's backside slumps to the left until he self-corrects.

"Shadow," I say a little louder now.

Godinez exchanges her leash with the big

guy, who now stands up. They both look in my direction.

Shady barks again.

"Shadow?"

He stumbles again, then regains his balance. His ears perk up. His nose points in my direction.

"Shadow," I scream.

He lets out that grumbling, gravely bark that would scare most, but which to me has always meant, "Yeah, it's me, and I'm here. What do you want?"

Godinez looks down at him, gives him a command, and they start coming. By the hangar, the buses rumble to life as they prepare to carry their cargo to a homecoming near you. Here behind the fence, I only have eyes for my Shadow. He steps with a faltering gait that becomes surer with each step. He's also got only eyes for me, nose for me, ears for me.

"Shadow," I shout now, wanting to believe I sound less hysterical than the last time I called his name.

He responds with the same bark and quickens his step. He barks again. His head points dead on at me as he approaches, now only a few steps away.

"Shadow," I say, my voice barely sounding out through a strangled throat.

He's here now, his nose less than an inch from me. I bend down as far as these legs will let me and grip the fence with my fingers. The fence is vibrating. No, I'm trembling.

"Shadow," I say.

He whimpers, and Shady comes close too and echoes him.

That's when it crashes over me. His eyes. Those eyes I loved looking into. Those eyes where his soul and mine met. Yes, because dogs have souls, no matter what one hundred theologians might say. I know they do. They have a soul. And now, as I long to look into his eyes, one shut like a sown up slit, the other clouded over, none of that mellow, tender brown to look into, I ask myself how I'll ever see his soul again. I wonder, too if that part of my own soul I entrusted to him is now also forever lost.

"Shadow," I cry out with a sharp, soft voice.

He whimpers, Shady whines, and I close my eyes.

"Shadow," I scream, hanging on the fence as my legs give out under me and I fall onto my knees.

Shadow growls and whimpers, and I hear him pawing at the fence as if he could cut through it.

"Jesus!" someone says beyond the fence.

"It's OK," a woman's voice says.

"Stand down," Brady says. I feel his heavy hand on my back, and it's the last thing I remember before I go all black.

Chapter 7

"That was a significant break for you," she says from behind the desk, her eyes judging me through them cute academia glasses, her body draped in that snow white coat.

My eyes fall on the brass name plate on her desk. "Dr. Taylor," it reads, same shrink that's been handling my case since I came back. I look down at my hands, bandaged. I try to bend my fingers. I guess I cut 'em up pretty bad, I'm thinking inside a head groggy with whatever cocktail they've had me on.

"How are you feeling?" she asks.

"Dazed. Doped up." For a few seconds I relive our last conversation, one we spent sparring about her wanting me to go on drugs, and me refusing to alter myself chemically. Bracing myself for a return to that unhappy topic, I tug at the edges of my bandages.

"Are you going to talk to me?" Taylor asks.

I look up at her. "What do you want me to say?"

"I just want you to share with me—"

"OK, I saw my dog come home. He's pretty banged up. I got emotional. Call me human, tell me how to be a better robot next time."

She looks down at my lap, at my hands. "Is that how you see it? Just a little emotional? Or is there something more to it?"

"It's just a dog. That it?"

"I know handlers and trainers form a bond with their animals."

"A bond."

"A special bond, I'm sure."

"A special bond. Do you even know what the hell you're talking about?"

"No, but you do, so why don't you tell me?"

"Those *bonds* risk their lives every day, just like any of us humans. Sometimes more."

"I've heard some amazing stories."

"Bet you have. Just like the amazing story you heard about some crazy chick flipping out when her dog came home."

"Care to elaborate?"

"Were you there?"

"There?"

"There when Shadow came home. There when I had the *significant break*. Were you there?"

"No, but I have the report."

"Bet you do. Just like them amazing stories you've heard. You read about 'em, and you think you have the whole story down pat. Is that how it works? That make any sense to you?"

"That's why we're talking. Because it's your story that matters."

"Oh, it does, now? That's so down right reassuring. Praise the Lord, I can tell my story."

She gives herself a minute to close her lips into a tight little circle. Glancing down at her notes, she says, "Your therapist's reports are very encouraging." She lifts her gaze. "Thank you for continuing to release them to us. It's very helpful."

"Very helpful to my gas mileage, too, so I don't have to trek it all the way down here every week."

"Yes, I suppose, since the sensitivity of your background can't be discussed *just* anywhere."

I shake my head at the stupidity of my arrangement, given that I can't discuss that sensitivity with my hometown therapist either. But whatever, I'm not going to bring that up and will keep being thankful they're willing to give me some leash, speaking of which, I'm guessing I need to sweeten up here pretty soon lest they shorten it right up for me.

"Well, and I'm real thankful I can have a full, flowing discussion with you today," I say.

Her head snaps just a bit at my sudden switch in demeanor. "Yes, of course. Full discussion is what we want."

"Look. I didn't go off on my family, like some PTSD dudes do. I didn't endanger anyone. I just had a moment. A good moment, I'd reckon."

"OK, tell me why it was a good moment."

"I let it all out. All the pain, all that Shadow means to me. I released it. I'll admit it wasn't pretty. I'll agree it was messy, but I needed to do that. To let it pour out. I'm not ashamed of it. I don't care what anybody thinks. I'm going to be honest with my emotions. I'm going to be transparent. Real. That's what I felt, that's who I am. Deal with it, or look the other way if you have to."

Not wanting to push things too far, I stop it there, look her straight in the eye. Go ahead, I'm defying her. Tell me why I'm wrong. Give me the textbook reason I should go on living like a repressed fake.

"That's good," she allows, though a hint of skepticism taints her voice. "But it's not just about your dog, is it?"

"Oh, you mean these?" I slap my knees. "That's going well. Haven't you heard? I can almost run a twelve minute mile. Might even make the Olympics, even if all I have to do for that is spin a couple of times and chuck a heavy-ass ball into the air, the farther the better."

"Yes, we are very happy with your physical progress. I hear those prosthetic legs are something special, too."

I slap my knees again. "Oh, yeah. A real wonder, the culmination of modern engineering."

"Your hikes are getting more ambitious." She flips a couple of pages. "That rescue after an unexpected late season snow storm. Very impressive."

"Snow shoes helped a lot."

She looks up at me, this time over the rim of her glasses. "You've always been a super fit person, but your ability to overcome your latest physical challenges is an inspiration to many, don't you think?"

"I guess."

"You don't see it that way?"

I turn away to look at the translucent drapes covering the one solitary office window. The sun's hitting them just right so that they glow almost pure white, or maybe it's my groggy eyes doing that.

"I'm sensing you struggle with that concept," she adds. "Why?"

There in the glow I ask myself, yeah, why is that? Why do I look at the whole way my heroism and physical impairment is being portrayed as nothing more than a marketing campaign? Why does it all seem so empty for me?

"You said you wanted to be real," she says. "Be real now. Be real with me."

"I'm damaged goods," I say.

"How so?"

"Never was much to look at or consider before I came into the Army. What little I became here, it's all broken now. Damaged." I turn to face her. "And I bet not even you can put it all back together, can you?"

"You're right. But we can talk about how you can move beyond that damage."

"Are you kidding?" I slap my thighs. "I'm literally carrying the damage with me every day, for the rest of my life."

"But that's not the damage we're talking about, is it?"

"Like I don't carry that too, every second, twenty-four seven."

She looks down at her papers again. With her eyes still there, her finger comes to rest on a particular spot of interest.

"Three days ago, during that rescue, why did you go up that mountain?"

I grin because she's walked into one of my favorite stock answers. "Because it was there."

She looks up with a grin of her own. "Sir Mallory, right?" She waits for me to answer, and when I don't, she asks. "Did that experience seem like any other you've had before?"

"I'm sure your file has the answer."

"I thought you wanted to be real with me."

"The with me part, I'm sure I never said that."

She leans back in her chair. "Why did you go up that mountain?"

"A young girl, a little boy and a dog tracking

her heart out. That simple. That straight-up. But I'm thinking you have fancier designs on it."

"As I'm sure your CO told you, we had some concerns about that."

"Brady," I say.

"Yes."

"Because it seemed too close to something else. Too similar. You didn't think I could handle it."

"Perhaps it would be helpful at this time to go through our exercise."

By this she means the monthly routine recounting of my PTSD inducing experience, the big one. Relive it, go through it blow by blow, face it for all its pain and anguish, and you get better. Or you get on top of it, like one gets on top of a snarling tiger, is more like it. You own it, and it doesn't make you blow up. Or so the wisdom goes.

My opinion? It hurts like hell at first. Then you go numb to it, and it doesn't much tilt things one way or the other. Well, maybe I have something to do with that, since after the first couple of recountings, I went home, cried myself through a full write-up, memorized it, and then spit it out like the flaccid, safe robot they want me to be.

I close my eyes, in keeping with how she's seen me do it in the past, and I do it now. I spit it out.

"We arrive at the village in the late afternoon. We come to look for IEDs. That's what the call said, anyway. When we get there, though, we find some sort of full-blown dispute. A lot of yelling. The villagers are all upset. The Marines are pushing them back. I'm thinking a riot's about to bust loose.

"Come to find out a family's been shot. A mom, a dad, and their oldest teenage son. One of the Marines tells us the son's an IED planter. *Was* an IED planter, he corrects himself. OK, where are the IEDs? I don't get an answer because World War three's breaking out, and who has time to answer stupid questions about IEDs.

"So while all that ruckus goes on, me,

Shadow and an interpreter we brought with us stay on the perimeter. I aim to see if I can find some of them IEDs on my own, and I go out to the main road, a goat trail, really, that leads out to the mountains. I figure that's a good place to start. We go slow, letting Shadow tell us if it's safe to walk on. He was great—"

I pause there. To camouflage the regurgitation, I usually change a couple of details. Pause and stammer for effect at different spots as the spirit leads. That makes it seem like I'm not going through the motions. This feels like a good point for the ad lib, though this one smacks me as more real. Something's really caught me short, namely the image of Shadow's ruined eyes.

"He is great. Can pick up an IED a football field away. Even found one covered with fresh goat meat. Could have made it goat droppings. Won't fool him any one way or the other."

"He is special," Dr. Taylor says, one of her usual quick bits of affirmation.

"As we're starting our search, a little boy

comes running to us. He's talking a mile a minute, but eventually the interpreter tells me a young girl and her little brother, daughter and son of the shot-up and dead family, they've run away, to them hills up yonder. Running away from the mean soldiers, the little guy says. Will I go find them. With my dog. He actually goes to pet Shadow, and I stop him because Shadow's working. So I release Shadow from his working stance, and I let the boy pet him, because that's something, I think. They hate dogs in that culture, and this little boy wants to pet one of the meanest looking ones."

I pause again and go through one of my usual heavy breathing bouts, like I'm about to lose it. Because this should be meaningful, you know, that little boy wanting to pet a supposed symbol of occupation. And because it is, all the way around, like Dr. Taylor and I rabbit-trailed in a prior discussion.

Her radio voice breaks the silence. "You're doing good."

"I ask the boy if we have anything that

belongs to either the boy or the girl. Some clothing, maybe. He and the interpreter jabber about it, and he runs off, comes back a minute later with a teddy bear. It's one of ours, the kind we give to the kids, because you know, a little toy from us is going to build up such good will even if we're shooting up their country."

I open my eyes to wipe them, because memorization or not, the tears still happen. I see her frowning down at her papers, and I confirm she noticed my last remark is a new addition. She's jotting it down, probably along with a note of hers saying I've developed doubts about the war, or something of that general persuasion.

I close my eyes again and go on.

"Shadow takes in the scent, and when I let him search he starts taking me up the mountain. At this point I stop and radio my CO for concurrence and support on the search. He's having none of it, but when I tell him that hey, finding those kids may earn us some goodwill with the villagers, he says he'll look into it."

"But there's another reason you want to go

up," she prompts.

"Yeah, a couple of months before, the MPs called in my services on a missing Afghan boy. We found him up a trail, strangled, a cross scratched on his forehead. Theories ranged anywhere from locals punishing his family for cooperating with us, to one of ours gone serial killer. I tracked him, found him, under a pile of rocks with an IED booby trapped around him. They were able to disarm the bomb to get to him, see the cross on his forehead, give the body back to the family."

"And at the village, you were thinking, ah, this could be another one."

"Yeah, but I don't tell no one that. I'm not an investigator, so I keep it simple. Just get those kids back, settle down the village. So we wait. That turns into hours, and pretty soon, as the sun starts setting, I know they're not going to clear us. And it's them Marines, having the lead on the operation that are putting the kibosh on it."

I open my eyes.

"So I get angry, leave Shadow with the interpreter, go marching off to give some bastard a piece of my mind, and as I'm walking by a goat cart, boom it goes, and there go my legs, too."

I look her in the eye now, hard and angry, knowing she won't much like how I abridged that last piece.

I cut off her impending objection with, "So I guess I see your point. Two kids, and as it turns out, an adult, run off to them hills. No one lets me go find them. Days later we find out they's dead, shot up by them Ta-li-ban nasty fellahs. And now fast-forward to present day Ame-ri-ca, and someone stops me again, though this time I have the dead body of a girl to count as a consolation prize."

"I am hearing some new issues we haven't touched on before."

"If my patriotism or loyalty to this country's what you're after, don't you lose no sleep over it. But yeah, there's some unexplored *issues* missing from your neat little files."

"Such as?"

"Such as I haven't relived everything for you. Such as *I* went back to the kids' hut, saw their shot-up parents and brother with mine own eyes, confronted the marine CO about going after those kids. Such as he snickered at me, called me a couple of politically incorrect names. Such as I popped him a good one. Such as that was too much for his honor, and he and two of his buddies gang-raped me to return the favor."

I pause to stand and lean over the desk, glaring down at her.

"Such as I stumbled out of that hut, beat and bloody, with a teddy bear in my hand. Such as that's when I stepped on the IED."

I leave out one last part, how lying on a hospital bed someone came to me and asked me some questions about the kid with the cross scratched on his head. Why? It turns out the boy that ran away from the village where I last walked on my God-made legs was found much the same way, even though in his case, no one thought him worth the effort and risk to disarm the IED, blowing him up and any evidence of a serial killer. Why do I leave that out? Because I didn't care on that bed, and I haven't cared for a long time, and the shame of putting my missing legs and my anguish ahead of those boys keeps me silent once again.

I look down at her papers, then back at her. "I don't see you writing, sister."

"This will require—"

"Adult supervision? Go ahead and get yourself some. While you're at it, tell the higher uppers this. You're going to let me go. With *my* dogs. I'm going to get in my SUV with both of them, the washed out bitch and the mangled stud. And we're going to drive up to my ranch in Fort Collins, and we're going to live happily ever after, whatever flavor of hell that ends up being for us, and you're going to stay out of our way. No more leash for Jane McMurtry. No more arrangement. It's over."

"I'm not sure that—"

"Or, I will use my newly found celeb to turn

your little op upside down. By the time I'm done with you, the inside of a latrine will seem pristine by comparison. Are you reading me clear, sister?"

I straighten out and take a step back. The chair behind me topples and tumbles backward, and I think to myself that's a nice touch, too.

What little color her already pale face had has vanished.

I point at her. "Do the right thing. If you still know what that is."

A minute later I'm walking outside, striding toward the kennel. It no longer feels familiar here. It feels like prison, and I aim to break out.

Chapter 8

It takes four hours for them to come see me. By them, I mean Brady, and Captain Select Casandra Godinez, who he brings along for solidarity. They find me in the kennel, where after unrolling a field sleeping bag on the floor, I've made a home of sorts in a cage with Shadow and Shady. It's silly, I know, but I don't have much experience with civil disobedience or the military variety, for that matter, so here you have it.

With fists on his waist Brady faces me down through the cage's gate. "What the hell do you think you're doing?"

"Pouting. Like the teenage daughter you always wanted."

He shakes his head at that, tries and fails to hold back a smile. "Looking for some fireworks?"

"Hmm. Fourth of July's come and gone."

"Well you ain't getting any. Sorry to disappoint."

He gestures to Godinez and she comes to unlock the gate. Though I stole a key, I was sure someone had a master, and it falls on her to do the honors.

"You can unlock that gate all you want," I tell them. "I ain't going anywhere."

As if to back me up, Shady takes a position between me and the gate. She growls her usual shy growl, but her stance takes me by surprise nonetheless. Shadow catches on a second later and joins her. His growl is less reassuring, especially to Godinez, who freezes before opening the gate.

"Jane, please, stop this," Brady says.

"Did you hear me give a command? Or do you think in just four hours I trained them to growl at the black guy and his Hispanic underling when I say 'I ain't going anywhere'?"

He rubs the back of his neck. "Wouldn't put it past you."

"I promise you. Look at them. I ain't the only one you guys have pissed off."

I let my words sit there, trading glances between Godinez and Brady. Something in her face tells me she's feeling caught in the middle, and I want to believe given the choice she'd take my side. As for Brady, he's smiling at me in a way that eases my tension.

I slap the floor. "Shady, Shadow, *hierr*." They come to me. Shady sits at my left, Shadow at my right.

"Now that's how I see you three," Brady says. "Back at that wonderful ranch of yours, sitting on the porch watching the fleas jump."

He turns to Godinez and adds, "Go ahead, open it up, and help them to the barracks and then to her car." He faces me. "That's right, McMurtry. You're free to go. Forever. Your stuff is packed, your sorry-ass SUV is in the parking lot. Make sure and write to let us know how your life as a dog goes."

With that, he walks off.

Godinez stands there, still frozen for a moment, until I say, "I promise I won't bite."

She smiles at that and unlatches the gate. Seconds later, I'm outside shaking her hand, joking with promises I haven't handled dog poop or pee.

We go through the motions, getting my stuff out of the barracks, changing back into my civilian clothes and leaving the loaner uniform I've been wearing. She walks me out, taking Shady while I lead Shadow. At the parking lot she helps me get them in the car. She does all this in relative silence, and when we're done, she takes a step back and salutes me.

"What the hell is that?" I say.

Godinez snaps her hand down and replies, "You know what it is."

Before I can conjure up a response, she's walking off, and I'm thinking maybe I would like to work with this girl.

We don't get too far down the road when I determine our seating arrangement ain't working. Shadow's too big for the back seat, takes up most of it, and Shady's having to sit the whole time while he slumbers. I should put her in the trunk, but she hates it back there, and I fear what little progress I've made in getting her to mind me will go out the window if I make her ride across three states in an arrangement she doesn't care for.

That leaves me with only one option. Though it's not the safest—illegal in some states, even—I bring her to the front passenger seat. At her size she'll have to sit there most of the time, unless I let her spread over my lap. Still, secured with her seat belt vest, she sits proud and tall. During short stretches, I place her in the back seat, while Shadow goes to the trunk. Along the way, I stop at a Walmart and buy a large padded bed which I should have thought to bring, and use that in the trunk for Shadow. I soon decide he loves that, so we make it a permanent accommodation: Shady in the back seat and Shadow in the trunk.

Left to me, I'd drive the whole way through with minimal stops to take care of basic biology. On account of Shadow's health and comfort, though, we make two overnight stays, the first at Amarillo, Texas, and the second at Colorado Springs, Colorado on the following night. I'm familiar with this route and know the motels that accept pets, even if my companions don't technically fall into that category.

When I push off from Colorado Springs and especially as I drive through Denver on I-25, the nagging thought that I should check in on Dan Murphy crosses my mind. More than cross, it assails it, really. I succeed in pushing it aside until I approach the junction for Highway 119, the last time when I can make a direct turn for Boulder, even if by now I'll be back-tracking somewhat. I go past 119 and pull over to make a call.

"Any luck?" I ask him after we get through

the front-end banter.

He doesn't answer right away, and the pause makes me think the worst.

"Not good news?" I ask.

"No, nothing like that. Same as last time we spoke."

"Oh." I want to add something stupid, like there's still hope, but it's been a long time. More than likely that boy is dead. For a moment I'm back in a dusty village, learning something along those lines while Shadow licks me in the face as if that can wash away my shame or extinguish my anger.

"How are you doing?" he asks.

"OK. Why do you ask?"

"Did your buddy get home OK?"

I look through the rear view mirror, half-expecting to see Shadow sit up, ears all perky. I hear him snoring instead.

"Yeah. You'll have to meet him sometime," I say, not really knowing why I've made that offer.

"Oh, is he local?"

I smile. "You could say that." I keep smiling, but in the end I decide I don't need to stay so coy. "He's coming home with me, actually."

"Oh," Dan replies, and I don't know whether I hear disappointment in his voice or want to imagine it.

"Is that jealousy I hear?" I ask, now kicking myself for flirting. Really? Again?

"It's none of my business, I guess."

"His name is Shadow," I tell him. "He walks on four legs, more or less like Shady."

He grunts something I figure for a curse. Or is it relief I hear in his voice?

"He was my dog over there. When I had to come home, he had to stay, finish his tour and all that. I wasn't supposed to get him until two years from now. But he got early release, if we can call it that."

"That's good, then," Dan puts in.

Something strangles my throat and I swallow to undo it. "More or less same reason I got sent home."

"Oh."

"He's snoring right now or I'd put him on the phone," I rush to add, my attempt to poke a pin through the balloon of our tension.

"Good, we all need our beauty sleep."

"Yeah, maybe," I say, and we both laugh it out.

When I tell him I need to go, he asks, "Where are you right now?"

"Just east of Longmont."

"How about we hook up there—" He clears his throat. "I mean meet, say, for lunch?"

Instinctively I look back, knowing I have an excuse there. After all, I have to get these two dogs home. They're tired, it's been a long drive, and what am I going to do with them while I bat eyelashes at a police officer over a lunch table? Perfect, right? It doesn't feel that way. Especially when Shady's looking up at me with an expression that says, "What are you waiting for girl?"

"To talk about your case?" I ask him.

"No, not really."

I swallow again. "Listen, Dan. I think by now

you know I'm pretty straight-up, right?"

"You can say that."

"So please don't take this the wrong way, OK?"

"OK."

I take a breath and go for it. "Would you really have much to do with a gal like me?"

"That's getting ahead of ourselves just a bit, ain't it?"

"Yeah, maybe."

His laughter sounds forced. "OK, here's me being straight-up with you. Yeah, I like you enough to want to know more about you. What happens after that, well, that's all maybe, right? Because we have to admit in life nothing's for sure."

"OK, I guess I can accept that."

"And?"

Another breath, and then, "I'm not that great to get to know, Dan. I have to lay that out there."

"I spent a day and a night with you on a cold mountain. I know you're prickly. Still. And?"

"It's more than that."

"I know."

"Do you?"

"Look, Jane. If this isn't a good time, I can take that. Main thing is to get you well."

The way he says this makes me wonder how much more he knows beyond my glaring blemishes and whatever is out on the media about PTSD and returning wounded veterans trying to make their way in life.

"You get yourself well," he adds. "That's mission one for you."

"Did they come asking questions?"

He hesitates. "If you mean your Army buddies, yeah, they did."

"What about?"

"Oh, they beat about the bush some. But I'm a cop. I can tell what they were after, why they were worried about you, just in the questions they asked. Especially when they put me on the phone with that chick, Taylor. Some kind of mind-gamer, that one."

I bite my lip. "Listen, Dan. I really need to

get going. These dogs, they're tired."

"Yeah, get home and get some rest. Maybe I'll call you later?"

"More straight-up for you. I'm going to need some time."

"Take it. All that you need."

We leave it there and hang up after saying our polite goodbyes.

I hear Shadow stir in the back, and Shady whimpers for good measure. I let them out for a bio break, and a few minutes later we're driving north again, aiming for a new life I'll have to sort out and they'll live as if nothing's up with the world.

Chapter 9

During the first week, Shadow and I feel each other out. Along with Shady we go for short, no more than half mile walks around the ranch. We do that twice, sometimes three times a day, depending on my schedule and how strong I sense Shadow's getting. Bum hind leg or not, he's enjoying himself. By the third day, I let him go off leash.

"Hell, boy, this whole place is yours, and you don't have to work it if you don't want to," I tell him more than once.

He seems to take to that gladly and does his best to keep up with Shady as she bounds through the tall yellow summer grass, a welcome relief to running on hot dust and rocky terrain, no doubt. His sight I judge as better than the ten percent assessment they gave me back at the base. Even with bad balance due to his hind leg, I don't see him stumbling and bumping into things. As for that leg, though I want to dismiss the impression as wishful thinking, I could swear it's getting stronger. Maybe with regular exercise in a non-stress environment it's getting less stiff.

At the end of that week I sense he's missing something, like he's at a loss. Maybe I'm reading in him what I feel in me. We all think we'd like the easy life, until we get the chance to wither in it.

That Sunday, after I come home from church I ask him, "You wanna work, don't you boy?"

He barks at me, and Shady backs him up with a rough bark of her own. In just one week, I think he's starting to rub off on her.

"Well, today's the Lord's day," I tell them. They look up at me, puzzled, as I guess a lot of people would these days were I to tell them the same thing. I explain, "We ain't in no war zone, so we do what he did when he was done creating us and this world he gave us. We rest."

They both bark at me, almost in unison, again, not because they understand my words, but because they get me.

Monday morning I step out before sunup to set up a scent track exercise. In the garage I find an empty flower pot and a couple of rags on which I sprinkle some of my gun powder. I set up one of the rags, the one with the most powder, out in the yard and hide it under the upside down flower pot. The other rag I drop in a zipped plastic bag I hide in my pocket.

When I'm done with that, I come back and have breakfast. By then, both Shady and Shadow are up, and dare I say, a little miffed I went out into God's country, even if in the cool of morning, without taking them along. Some high protein kibble in their bowls earns me some quick forgiveness. When I'm done with my toast and eggs, they follow me to the bathroom because apparently, watching me brush my teeth fascinates them. Once that show's over, we head outside.

I tell myself again, as I've been telling myself since yesterday, that this will be an easy exercise. No fast running, no jumping. Just shaking off the dust to see where things stand.

They're both looking at me with expectation dripping from their tongues when the sound of rubber on gravel draws our combined attention. A cloud of dust wafts up behind a powder blue 1950s Ford pickup truck. I know at once who's coming: Allison Holtz, itinerant Vet, the kind that tends to ailing animals, as opposed to the kind that comes home all shot-up and in need of some medical and/or psychological TLC.

She and I have had a sputtering friendship. When I first moved here from my hometown in Wyoming, we struck a quick birds of a feather relationship. Maybe with my expertise in dogs and her recently minted Veterinarian degree, together we could do something special, out of the box—beyond the box, as she put it. Something a bit more interesting than me breeding and training dogs and her swapping horseshoes and filing hooves. We kicked a few innovative ideas around—innovative mostly on her account, I must admit—but nothing came of it.

At some point I got a whiff that she played for the all-girls team, and that unsettled me enough to put some distance between us. Not that I'm going to look down my nose at anybody because of that. Surely I learned to live and get along in the Army. But I wasn't raised like that. Though I'm not going to discriminate anyone on that account, certainly won't seek to hurt them, I have my rights too, like who I associate with, and what ideas I give them about my availability and desirability.

In the end, we stayed cordial. I actually invited her to church, and to her credit and my respect, she came. Not only that, but she attends once or twice here and there, depending on star and satellite alignments, I venture to guess. She also looks after Shady for me, medically and with boarding at her own house during weeks when I go do my reservist and/or psychoanalysis duty down in Lackland and don't want to lug my rebellious teenager along.

"Hey, Shady!" Allison says as she walks to us. Per her M.O., animals get greeted first.

Shady is already at the fence, standing on her hind legs, front paws draped over the top. Shadow goes in that direction, then stops and sits. Allison, already coming around the yard entrance, with Shady bounding up next to her, goes for him next.

"And could this be the famous—"

One of them scariest growling, base of the Opera barks I haven't heard from him since the war comes gushing out of his throat and through his teeth.

For a moment I'm tempted to see how Allison handles it, walking up to an animal she's treating like a pet when she should look upon him as a loaded weapon. But that ain't fair. Besides, Shadow should know better than that. He's not in work mode, and he shouldn't... Oh, wait, I was about to work him, he knows that, and it's Shady that broke protocol, as usual.

I run to him, grab him by the collar and tell him to sit. Which seems on the face of it stupid since he's already sitting, but after some petting, I get him to realize he can go back into sociable mode.

"It's OK now," I tell Allison. "My bad. I was about to exercise them and —"

"I can see how he saved your life." She comes closer, extends her hand to him palm down. When he's done sniffing, she looks up at me. "Tell me what to do."

"You can pet him."

"Get down at his level OK?"

"Relax. He's not a murdering wolf."

Allison kneels down and puts both hands on his chest. At 5′ 1″, on her knees she looks like a midget next to Shadow. He leans forward and sniffs her red hair, finally laying one long lick of his tongue on her freckled forehead.

"You're in," I say.

"God, Jane! He's beautiful! All black, just about. Never seen one like him, this big, this black, this... studly. There, I said it!"

"He's gained a little weight since—." I have to cut myself off there. "We'll lean him out again, get him to all muscle. Right, Shadow?"

He lets out a bark, a happier one this time, but the power of it still throws Allison back on her butt. She's startled at first, then starts laughing, goes down on one elbow, and that only invites Shady to join the fun, while Shadow sniffs on. I let that horsing around go on for a minute or so before I break it up.

"Got some coffee inside," I tell Allison. "Want some?"

"Sure, but you were about to exercise him, you said? I don't want to cut in on that."

"You wanna see?"

"Are you kidding? Yeah, I want to see."

"Nothing you haven't seen me do with Shady."

"Yeah, but this is Shadow." She back-slaps me on the upper arm. "Come on, don't be a stiff. Show me how this beautiful monster gets it done." Allison side-steps toward me. "But first, tell me where to stand."

"Right there is fine. It's just a scent track test, OK?"

"OK."

I call them both over, explain to Allison I'm doing a side-by-side, to see which of them is quicker, and then I take a cloth out of my jacket. I let them both smell it, counting off the same number of seconds to give them the same exposure.

At my command, Shady bounds off in no particular direction, and I fear this won't be much of a control. She's in one of her let's play modes. Shadow stands for a moment, surveying the air with his nose. Then he trots off in no particular hurry, straight for where I hid the prize.

"I see a little limp," Allison whispers. "But he's moving really well."

Within a few yards of the pot he slows down. At first, I think maybe his bad leg is bothering him, but with each stride he slows down even more until he's slinking toward it, stalking it, freezing with his chest now low to the ground.

"Come on," I whisper. "You got it. You know it's there."

But my willing him to move does nothing. He won't budge. I'm starting to think I need to go over to correct when from his left Shady comes barreling in, knocks over the upside down flower pot I used to conceal the prize, grabs the rag, and speeds to me, though when she gets to us, she shoves her snout in Allison's hand.

Allison looks up at me, holding up the rag, "Sorry," she says. "Is this OK?"

"Yeah, maybe."

I'm looking at Shadow, and he's half-turned back to me, looking at me with his one eye. Inside its foggy haze I want to think he's saying he's sorry. Truth be told, I see something else. Fear.

"Good job, Shady!" Allison is saying. "Oh, I'm probably not supposed to say that? It's not my place, sorry. It's not my place, right?"

I'm already two, three steps back toward the house. Inside I brew another pot of a Vanilla flavored coffee I know Allison likes. To her credit, she waits me out without saying anything else. When I go out to the porch, she's sitting on one of the rocker chairs with Shady next to her.

Shadow's lying in the middle of the yard, staring at the toppled flower pot. He turns to me again when he hears me come out. I set the two coffee mugs on a teak table between Allison's rocker and the one I will sit on. With some reluctance, I turn toward Shadow again.

"*Hierr!*" I call out to him, hating how harsh and angry my voice sounds.

He trots, limping more now, or maybe I'm imagining it. He climbs the four steps onto the wooden porch and comes to stand by me. I sit on the rocker before I totally lose it. With a pull on his collar, I draw him closer to me. He exhales a quick snort.

"It's OK," I whisper, and when he whimpers back at me, I squeeze my eyes shut and try my best to breathe. I feel Allison's hand on my shoulder.

"Maybe he needs more time," she says. "That's all. You understand that and him better than anybody else. Time will get it done."

"Yeah," I whisper. I reopen my eyes and to him I say, "I'm sorry. I'm sorry, boy. It's not your fault."

In his eye, even in the cloudiness of it, he's telling me he doesn't hold me responsible.

"No one needs to be sorry here," Allison says, as if translating for Shadow. "Let's all take a break, hang out, sip some delicious coffee, look out at the Colorado grass getting yellower, and then we'll figure out what to do with the rest of our day."

I look over at her and say, "Thank you."

"No, thank you for remembering my favorite flavor." She raises her cup. "Hey, I have an idea. After we chill out for a bit, let's take big boy over there to the hospital. I'll look him over, maybe run an MRI and such."

"I don't know. Not today."

"You said you'd let me do it. He's been here a whole week, and all I've gotten is the faxed medical stuff from you. Come on, on me, my treat."

I look back at Shadow and for some reason in his expression I read I should let her do it, or else, she'll never shut up.

"Thanks," I tell Allison. "Whenever it's good for you."

Chapter 10

After some unconvincing objections on her part, I prevail on Allison that in exchange for her examination of Shadow, I'll cook her lunch. I'd like to think my bit about leaving her non-green truck at my place and carpooling in my slightly greener clunker to her hospital clinches the deal, too, but that's wishful thinking.

Either way, she grabs her medical bag out of her truck, and we all pile into my 4Runner. Twenty minutes later we arrive at the university, where as part of the veterinary program, she shares privileges to the lab. A sweet deal for her. She can have a home office, a roaming one out of her truck, and do all the heavy lifting at the university at minimal to no cost to her. In exchange, she mentors students and takes them around her rounds to get them experience. Win-win for everybody. For her operations—she told me on the way here she has two today, starting at two in the afternoon— Allison charges her clients to offset costs, for which she makes payment to the university. Students tag along there, too, and get hands-on training. Double win-win for everybody.

Once inside, we get access to the MRI lab without problem, just as she promised. I convince her we don't need to sedate Shadow. Allison's not used to that. I tell her if I command him to lay still, he will do it even with bombs blowing up around him. She shakes her head at my claim and says that, OK, she'll try it.

Shadow proves me true and makes a believer out of her.

"Think of all the money we'd save on anesthesia," she tells me.

A couple of minutes later, with Shady and Shadow sprawled on the floor, I look over Allison's shoulder as she examines the MRI slices she took of Shadow's right hind leg and upper joint. It is at that joint that she stops, tapping on the screen several times.

"I've no idea what this is," Allison says after replaying the MRI sequence.

"What do you mean?"

"I'm pretty up on all the latest reparative joint techniques and sockets out there. This is not one of them, Jane."

I straighten up and have to force myself to keep breathing. "Huh. That's weird."

"Yeah, I mean, look at this. It almost looks like... A gear? Yeah, a gear, right? Some sort of mechanism?" She looks up at me. "The military did this?"

I freeze for a moment before I snap out of it. "Ah, look, do me a favor? Let's just go ahead and delete those files. Can we do that?"

"Why—"

"Just... trust me. Let's just make believe we didn't see that, OK? No more questions, not here, anyway? You can do that for me, right Allison? Like now?"

She frowns then scowls at me. "What the hell?"

"Please."

I'm thinking of what else we might need to do. Our phones? We left those outside because their signal might interfere with the equipment. Check. No one would have known to pre-bug this place because we came here on a whim. Check. What else? The files. That's all. They need to go, and we need to make sure that any copies, temporary or otherwise, go away too. Permanently. Then, I need to take care of Allison. She'll want answers, and I'll need her strict discretion. But how much can or should I tell her?

"Talk to me, Jane. You're freaking me out."

"Please. Just delete everything." I look into her blue eyes, and I make a quick call. "I'll tell you everything, but those files, whatever this machine recorded, they need to go. All of them."

She frowns at me, grabs a handful of her red hair, and then she turns to the computer screen. On it she commands deletion of the full MRI record. After that, she reaches for the phone.

"Hey, Rob, yeah, Allison here. Listen, I made a boo-boo. I deleted some test MRI files. No biggie if they're gone, but I was wondering if there are any copies I can use to recover." She listens. "Yeah, really recent files, created less than an hour ago." She listens again. "Ah, shoot. That's kind of what I was afraid of. What about temp files?" A pause. "Nah, I can do it, just give me the directory and I'll check it out." She types as she listens to him, phone tucked under her neck. "Thanks, I'll give that a try. But if it doesn't work, no biggie. It was a simple test, and I can re-run it."

She hangs up and winks at me. "Almost there." On the screen she lists a bunch of files. With her finger she scans the time stamps. "Ooops, nothing before 5:40 PM last night, the last time anyone used this dumb machine." I see her scanning a couple of other directories around the one the IT guy gave her. "Nope, nothing there either."

Allison turns in her chair and looks up at me

with a coquettish smile. "Now let's go back to your ranch for some interesting story time, shall we?"

On the drive back, Allison tries to get a head start on story time. I tell her no, not now, not here. She grows serious at that.

A mile or so later, she asks, "Shadow really froze this morning, didn't he?"

"I was there."

"You can hardly blame him."

"I know that."

"Maybe you shouldn't try to work him anymore. Maybe he should just retire."

"He's five. And he's too driven. Dogs like him don't do early retirement."

"Come, on, Jane. Every time he goes sniffing for something, he's going to think it's a bomb. Wouldn't you?"

"We get over those things. We keep going. He will, too. You just wait and see. That dog is one tough piece of canine. He ain't gonna roll over and just give up."

"I'm not talking about giving up on him or him giving up. Just that—"

"It ain't who he is. He ain't built, and here I mean on the inside, to be prancing around some farm the rest of his life, smelling flowers and chasing butterflies." I look back through the rear view mirror expecting to see him there. I don't, so I suppose he's napping again, back there on his soft new trunk bed. "That dog's a fighter, and if you coddle him, he'll wither from the inside out. Reason I worked him is because I felt him floundering, like he's searching for something to do."

"OK, we all love animals, but you're humanizing him, now."

I turn to stare her down. "You don't know'im like I do, Allison."

"Alright, you're right." She waves her hands and looks away.

We arrive at the ranch shortly after 10 AM, with plenty of time for stories, followed by lunch, and a little bit of margin for Allison to make it back into town for her 2 PM operation appointment.

Allison stays back with the dogs and gets them out of the car while I go in the house. I come out with a pair of binoculars which immediately earn me a couple of strange looks, one from Allison, the other from Shady. I get one more of those looks when I tell Allison to leave her cellphone behind.

"Let's go for a walk," I say once we're all set.

With the dogs off leash and leading the way after I point them in the right direction, we take a narrow trail that curls around the house, out to the back yard and through a grove of thin Aspens. Beyond the grove, the trail widens a bit and winds through a grassy field, rising up to a small hill, where another grove of Aspens awaits us.

Though we've talked about it plenty, I've never taken Allison on a tour of the property. She's more or less seen the house, the front yard, and a barn that stands to the south of the house.

She's never seen this western part, or what lies beyond it. As if forgetting why we're going for a walk, she starts oohing and aahing about the grounds.

"Man, how lucky are you that your dad left you this land," she says. "You say your dad did some cattle ranching here?"

In the past I've told her how my dad's side of the family is from Missouri, where somewhere around Westplains they did some cattle ranching. A couple of generations into it, there were enough brothers to make things a tad crowded, so some of them moved out west. My dad ended up in Wyoming, where he married and where I was born. Sometime around his fifties, when I was still in high school, he got this idea to buy some land further south, and this is the ranch he picked up for a song, as he told the story.

The new property would allow him to diversify. He made a go of it for a couple of years, then gave up, never getting around to sell the land. My guess? Doing so would force him to make a final admission of error. Plus I like to believe Dad wanted to leave one piece of land to my brother, and the other to me, even if he never made that terribly clear.

"So your brother kept the ranch in Wyoming?" Allison asks.

"Yup. Really wanted to sell this one. Was almost set on it, until I came back from my last tour. He let me have it for another song." I don't add because it was his way to feel sorry for me and get my depressed, crippled butt away from him. But that's not a kind thing to say, so I leave it between Shady and me, as I've told her plenty, especially after a couple of beers.

"Well, you're super lucky. I think it's great for people to tend to the land. It's the one thing that grounds us, you know?"

"Yeah, maybe."

We walk a little farther through the field. It's warm, here in late August, and what breeze blows doesn't give much relief. We're all glad when we reach the trees and the shade they provide.

"OK, this is good." I'm looking through the binoculars, scanning all the way around. I don't see anything or anyone.

"Here's where I'm going to look a little paranoid," I tell Allison. "But it's just precautionary. Call it belt and suspenders."

"Would the belt be why we're not talking at your house? Why we left our phones there?"

"Yup. And this here is the suspenders."

I do a full three-sixty scan one more time before I stand each dog facing key locations from which I would be watching if I were doing the surveillance I hope no one is doing. I place them at almost ninety degrees to each other, facing more or less in the direction of the house and the road that leads into it. Out of kindness, I make sure they're under the edge of the shade and gauge it will last long enough.

To each I give the watch command, *"Pass Op."*

I come back inside the grove to find Allison shaking her head.

"You're right about the paranoid part," she

says. "Thing is, I'm feeling it too. What the hell was that thing in Shadow, Jane? Some experimental, military bionic gadget?"

"Here's the truth, Allison. I don't really know."

"You said you were going to tell me."

"I don't know, but I can guess."

"An educated guess."

"Yeah. Rumor had it with all the busted vets coming home with missing body parts, the Department of Defense funded research into making them whole. At least insofar as is needed to bring'em up to fighting standards, that is."

"You mean—"

"Recent wars, more than any others have saved lots of lives. Problem is, people come back pretty messed up. It depletes the force, too. Many soldiers would jump at the chance of getting put back together and going back for another tour. So they started working on a solution. Maybe they're trying it out on injured dogs, a problem of its own."

"You're blowing me."

"Again, just a rumor." I make sure I have her full attention, as if that's necessary. "Here's the thing, Allison. We're not supposed to know. You, me, we're not cleared for this information."

"We'll, we know it now."

"No, we don't. We saw some gadget inside a dog. That's all. Part of me didn't want to tell you anything, but then you might go talking to some reporter, and next thing you know—"

"They'll shoot me."

"It ain't that simple. Shooting might be a kindness."

"Thanks."

"Listen, Allison. Just. Keep. Your. Mouth. Shut. Trust me on this."

She squints at me. "Are you sure you don't know more than you're letting on?"

"I'm leveling with you."

She narrows her eyes as if that lets her read me in full. When she's done with that, she asks, "Then why would they release Shadow to you, with a ticking secret government project inside him?"

Her question stuns me. Why would they risk it? Surely they might guess I might take Shadow to a Veterinarian, maybe take an X-ray, or even an MRI. Then I would know. Someone else might know, too.

"I don't know," I reply.

"It's an answer worth knowing, don't you think?"

"We agree there."

I take my binoculars to scan the surroundings again. From here it's a waste of time, since the trees block segments of my view. But passing time is what I need right now to try and divine some sort of answer.

"Hey, Jane. Out on a limb question here. Do you think your legs are part of the same project?"

I turn to her with a frown. "You kidding, right?"

"When I first read that you're running and hiking miles, I did a little Google searching. Blade runner notwithstanding, your legs, the way you walk and move with your *special* ones, it's really outside the norm."

I fight the urge to get defensive, but still say, "That took a lot of physical therapy. I nearly killed myself to get to where I am."

"Not to take away from you or your hard work, Jane. But don't you think there's been at least one other person out there who's done the same? Worked as hard? Yet, somehow, you're the only one hiking up mountain trails, running 5Ks with a near natural gait, and training for the Olympic trials."

"Sounds like a nice theory, but it's not the same as Shadow. I don't have some gears in me."

"Maybe you don't need it." She points at my legs. "Maybe it's good enough to have it on you. Let me tell you what. How about we use the scientific method?"

"Huh?"

"We formulate a hypothesis then we test it. Here's one: if we take one of your good legs apart, in particular that smoothly articulating ankle, we'll find gearing similar to what we saw in Shadow's hip. Too bad we don't have a full set of pictures of those, but we can remedy that easy enough."

"This is crazy, Allison."

"Yeah. Crazy enough to be hiding among some Aspens while two dogs stand watch to make sure no one's listening to us with remote parabolic dish microphones."

"What?"

"Yeah, you're the badass military operative, but me? I kill a lot of time online reading ridiculous conspiracy theories."

I'm about to respond when I hear Shadow let out one, short bark. With my binoculars, I look where he's looking. I see a white SUV driving up the road to my house.

"Yeah, this is some kind of crazy, alright," Allison whispers next to me. "Next up, how did Shadow see that with that bad eye of his?"

"He heard it or smelled it," I suggest.

"Did he?"

I sigh. There's no sense in arguing. Truth of it

is, I'm not so sure she ain't right.

Chapter 11

By the time we get closer to the house I'm relieved on at least one count. Through the binoculars I recognize Dan Murphy's SUV. He stands next to it, looking annoyed that while he can see two cars in front of the house, one of them with a hood still warm to the touch, he can't find any humans to go with them.

Without phones on us I can't call him to let him know we're here. I break into a jog for fear he'll leave before we get to him. Shady takes my cue, and sprints ahead, reaching him first. By the time we arrive at the front of the house, a tad winded and a lot sweaty, Dan and Shady are having a good time going at it with one of her tug-of-war chew toys.

"There you are," he says to us, a little winded himself after his short romp with Shady.

I do the introductions, Allison first, then Shadow.

"God, he's a monster," Dan says. "If I had seen you coming with him, I would have run the other way."

"You should have run the other way all the same," I reply, and the three humans laugh together.

We go inside the house, where I start working on lunch. I leave the what brings him here question unasked, both for fear of what it might bring up about the search he and I couldn't finish on that mountain, and because if it has nothing to do with that, I'm not sure he or I want to get into it with Allison there.

But that's how I feel about it, and if Dan doesn't, I figure he'll take corrective action all on his own. If it's urgent, he'll bring it up. But he doesn't, not straight away. He lets us settle into lunch preparation before he comes around to it, just as I'm about to pour the water from the boiling pasta pot.

"Have you seen CNN today?" he asks.

"Can't say that I have," I say.

Allison raises her hand. "I have."

"Big story about Boulder," Dan adds.

"Yeah, the one about the missing boy and his dead sister."

I pour the water and pasta into a caldron and avert my face from the rising steam. "Did they find 'im?"

"Not yet." Dan clears his throat. "What the story didn't cover, there's another kid missing. Another boy, about the same age, very similar look." He pauses for a second to add, "We should probably talk about it after lunch."

"Why?" I ask. "Because lunch ain't ruined already?"

"Doesn't look ruined to me," Allison says waving her nose over the red sauce. "Smells delicious, don't it Dan?"

He looks at me, and I get his meaning.

"We should probably talk about it in private," I say. "Police business and all that."

Allison makes a face. "Sure. Why not? Besides, who can trust me with a secret, anyway?"

I want to throttle her for that, but I don't want the sauce to overcook, so I set to finish that task before dealing with her. How I'll do that, I have no idea.

To keep her occupied, I give her a tomato to chop for the salad. By the time she's done with that red fruit of the vine, lunch is ready.

"So how did you two meet?" she says before anyone's taken a bite.

"Jane helped us track during a search and rescue." Dan looks over at me to let me know he's got this. "She and I found the dead girl."

"Wow. That's some drama and trauma right there," Allison says, looking mostly in my direction. "How long did it take you?"

"A few hours," Dan replies.

Still looking at me, she presses on. "Lost the trail on the boy?"

I shove a spoonful of lettuce into my mouth.

Dan says, "We thought we had something,

but had to call off the search the next day. Jane had another commitment, down in Texas, so she could no longer aid our effort."

"Shadow?" Allison asks me.

I nod.

"Well, it looks like the case is heating up again," Allison adds. "Warmer trails to track." She gives me a sideways, upraised eyebrow look. "You're not thinking of taking Shadow, are you?"

With lettuce still left to chew, I go on and do the impolite thing anyways. "I'm not thinking anything at the moment. The man hasn't even told me what he wants."

"With all due respect, why else would he come all the way up here from Boulder if not to ask you to track something, you know, like with a dog?" She takes out her cellphone and shows me the screen. "The latest boy to go missing? They're looking for him at Estees Park. My guess? The good deputy here wants to shoot across on Highway 36 to lend a hand, preferably with you along for the ride."

"And if he does, he and I will discuss that after we've had our nice lunch." I glare at her.

She shrugs. "Just saying. If you do go, Shadow should stay. I can take care of him."

"Thank you. I'll take that under advisement. Now, please, do enjoy your pasta. You have two big operations waiting for you this afternoon, and we wouldn't want them patients suffering on account of your malnutrition."

"Look, I'm sorry, Jane. I guess I get a little excited when a friend of mine is involved in a big case. Network news and all. And I'm concerned for Shadow."

"I know."

We eat for a few minutes without another word. A senior officer once told me silence forms a vacuum the speech of the weak minded inevitably fills. Sounds like a quote from someone with keen insight into the human psyche, because I've seen it fulfilled often. I sit there, wondering which of us will show weakness first, and with what manner of inane or substantive remark. I end up deciding none of us fall into the category, as minute after minute goes by with no one getting sucked into the vacuum. Even the dogs, having trashed their own lunch bowls as we eat, keep to themselves, each in a corner of the kitchen, Shady alert, Shadow slumbering with his head turned and resting against his front paws.

"That was pretty good," Allison says as she excuses herself to leave. "I'll leave you two to your business."

I'm starting to rinse the dishes when she pulls away. Dan is watching her also, his arm propped against the kitchen window sill. I catch a glimpse of him, standing there and looking out to the property, and for a second I allow myself to wonder what it would be like to have him or someone like him do that on a regular basis, right here, sharing my kitchen and the life that goes with it.

"Allison's right," he says turning to me. "You're a pretty good cook."

"Yeah, and I like the way you shoe-horned your way into me cooking you lunch. I'll warn you, though. Dinner's a much tougher ordeal."

He smiles at me. I smile back. I like that moment. I like the way we smile at each other, simple, not awkward, not full of expectation or pretense or any of the other consenting deception that goes on with the mating dance people doodle around each other.

I set the rest of the dishes in the sink, turn off the water, and return to the table.

"What do you have for me?" I ask him after I retake my seat.

He comes over and sits across from me. "Allison's right about that, too."

"Yup. She's sharp that way."

"Except I don't want to go to Estees."

"Huh."

"I don't think it's the same case. We don't have to go into why, but there's something I want you check out back in Boulder. Something I found a couple of days after you left."

"What's that?"

"A semi-abandoned vehicle, parked at the other end of the trail we were following, on the other side of that ridge where we left off."

"Sounds interesting."

"Yeah, get this. An old Bronco, windows rolled all the way up, so it's sealed in there, and covered in camouflage netting plus whatever twigs and branches the owner could find. No plates, I'm guessing stolen, so tracing it won't lead anywhere."

"You think it's the getaway vehicle."

"You catch on quick. If I'm right, that's how the perp took the boy out of there. Brought it back. Left it."

"Why would he risk that? I'd dump it somewhere else."

"It's a long shot, I admit. So here's my question for you. To confirm it, we'd need to know whether that boy was in there. I don't want to go the whole nine yards, impound to see if we get a DNA hit and all that. I want it there, for when he returns."

"Because you think he'll use it again."

"Yeah, if he planned to use it once, he'd dump it somewhere else. Instead, if this is the vehicle, he brought it back and took great care to hide it."

"That's a lot of if-and-then hops."

"All of which become yes or no with a sniff inside the cab. If that's something that would work."

I absorb that for a moment. "It could work. Depending on how long the boy was in there, whether the windows were rolled down during travel, if anyone took the time to clean the interior, how hot and cold it's gotten inside the vehicle from sitting out in the open. All the same, it's worth a try. You got a warrant yet?"

"Shouldn't really need one. I'm not looking for evidence, just confirmation. We get a positive, all we gotta do is sit on the Bronco until our perp shows up. All the same, a warrant should be in place in a couple of hours. Worked it on the way here."

"Hope you got someone with eyes on that Bronco now."

"I'm afraid I don't."

"That's a bad wrinkle."

"I know," he says.

"So we need to move."

"I'll drive, siren on, all the way down."

I look over at Shadow. I know I should leave him, but if we need to get down to Boulder on the double, I can't board him with Allison until evening, after she gets off work. But that don't supply sufficient excuse. After all, I could find alternative arrangements with a local kennel easy enough.

No, more than anything, I don't want to separate myself from him. We've done enough of that already. I'm also expecting to find something very faint inside that Bronco, long dissipated by a number of circumstances like the ones I rattled off to Dan. I need Shadow's nose. He may be gun shy, but he knew that flower pot had the scent from yards away, clear across the yard.

"OK," I say.

"He's going, isn't he?"

"Oh, yeah." I look up to face Dan. "You know, you could've just called."

He shrugs. "But then I wouldn't have scored a free lunch."

I smile back at him and notice he's not doing the same.

"You sure you're up to this, Jane?"

I look back at Shadow and wonder how ready either of us is to go tracking. "There's baby steps and there's steps of faith," I say. "Sometimes they amount to the same thing."

Chapter 12

We spend the next half hour packing. Because I'm used to taking off with less than a day's notice, I have what I and the dogs need for the trip at hand, neatly stacked in the garage. Dan helps me stow food, water, my backpack, and of course, my new addition, Shadow's fluffy bed which fits even better in the back of Dan's Tahoe. With all that, by 1:45 PM we're on I-25 speeding south, lights flashing up top.

Dan makes some not so small talk during the first few minutes. He tells me about his plans, how he doesn't want to be a grunt cop all his life. To that end, he's going to the University of Colorado, getting a criminology degree. He's a little fuzzy about it until I push, and he finally cops—pun intended—to going for a PhD. I harass him a little about that, and when I'm done I ask him what the world he wants with a PhD degree. A little more cajoling, and he confesses—that's how it comes across—he'd like to work for the FBI.

What about me, he asks? Don't the Army pay for one's education, GI bill and all? Now it's my time to confess that I'm a hands-on learner. I much rather open up a manual, do as I go, and presto, there's my learning. That's how I did it in the Army, how I got along with dogs. From hand to brain, that's how I get things, back to hand, rinse, repeat.

"But you do have a college degree, don't you?" he asks.

"Oh, yeah." I pause for effect as I turn to him with a grin. "English major. That explain things for ya?"

"Not quite what I would have expected."

"I wanted to go in as an officer, not an enlisted grunt, and since as a little girl I was a reader, I figured, heck, maybe comparative literature. The reading was OK, except for all them old books written in foreign languages claiming to be old English. As you may guess, essay writing was not my forte. I didn't so much graduate as managed to escape from college. Got out of there with a degree suitable for framing by the barest of margins."

He smiles at that, but not too hard, probably for fear I'll take it as dissing of my limited, now PTSD-infected intellect.

"I'd say you've done well for yourself," he comes back after a long silence. "Expert in your field."

"Oh? How do you figure that?"

He pauses before saying, "That's what your Lieutenant Colonel said." Another pause. "Called me last night." One more pause. "Returned my call, actually."

This should unsettle me, but the comfortable plush seat and the vibration of the road under me bring on a relaxing effect, even make me a bit drowsy.

"You know that's how dogs learn, too, don't

ya," I say.

"What?"

"Hands-on, or paws-on as it were. You show them, you make them do, repeat it at least three times, reinforce with rewards and praise along the way. That's how Shadow back there became an expert in his field."

"I guess that's one way of looking at it."

We leave it at that. He doesn't push any further into my education or disdain thereof. I avoid poking around the dung field of why he would call Brady to get permission to see me and bring me back into the investigation. After all, I can guess why: fragile, handle with care, don't bend her too far, or God knows what the big crazy chick might do.

I lean the seat back, close my eyes and sink into the leather.

The rattling of the dashboard and the bouncing of the vehicle under me rouses me from sleep, roughly forty-five minutes later. We're on a dirt trail, winding upwards among fields of yellow-tan grass. Up ahead and to the right, I see some rock formations rising up from the valley floor, and I guess they're the flipside of whatever we were climbing a few days back.

In the back seat and trunk, both Shady and Shadow stir with whistle-like whining. More than once Shadow snorts, the way he does before a job, like he's clearing his nasal passages of any gunk that will get in the way of his ability to pick up the scent. I say a couple of things to calm them down, to make them less tense, but both dogs remain on edge.

Dan seems pretty tense himself. As he drives, he scans the surroundings. Ahead the trail bends to the right around some trees. Dan parks on the right, just shy of the turn.

"We go on foot from here," he says.

Outside, he tells me and the dogs to stand to the side while he lays some large branches along the side and back of his Tahoe to conceal it. But there ain't enough branches to make a credible job of it. Anybody coming down the road will pick it out easy enough, but I don't say it. He's the one on the verge of a PhD.

When he's satisfied, he tells me to stay with the dogs inside the shade line the trees cast. He'll come back in a second. I watch him slink among the trees as far as he can go, then make his way around the bend until I lose sight of him.

"I think we're clear," he says when he comes back a minute later.

I walk out and hand him Shady's leash. He leads with her. At first he has trouble with her lurching forward until I teach him the command for heel, and she decides to mind it.

Shadow and I follow. We go slow. I tell Dan he can go faster if he wants, but he doesn't, probably figuring I don't want to push Shadow too hard. The trail rises at a gradual, easy grade, and I think God for that. I also thank Him when Dan tells me it won't be far, a little under a half mile by his estimation.

Dan looks back several times as we move along. "You know he's not limping, right?" he says after the fifth or sixth look.

"Must be having a good day," I reply

wondering whether it has more to do with that contraption holding Shadow's hip together.

We walk for a few more minutes until we see it. Whoever concealed it did a much better job than Dan did with his SUV. I only pick it out because I'm looking for it. Confirmation comes when Dan points it out. There it is, wedged into another grove of trees that butts against the base of the rising cliffs.

As we near it, I look up to the rocks, a compilation of stacked boulders and jagged rock face, and I want to ask how anybody got down on that. I guess Dan will tell me soon enough. But right now he's handing me Shady's leash so he can go to work clearing up one side of the camouflage around the vehicle.

Once he's just about cleared the driver side door, he unloads his backpack. I expect him to take out a tool for unlocking the car, but instead he comes out with a clear evidence bag. Though it's folded and crumpled up, I recognize the boy's Spiderman T-shirt. He hands it to me.

"Get a whiff before I open the door?" he

asks.

I nod, open the bag and let Shadow smell the shirt. Shady comes over to inspect the marker, but I shoo her away. When I'm satisfied I look up at Dan and nod.

He grabs the handle and opens the door. I lead Shadow up to it. Without my prompting, he jumps right up. His voluntary willingness surprises me, as does the agility with which he made the leap. In another second he's full on at work in there, sniffing every surface, climbing into the back.

I poke my head in to watch him, and tears well up in my eyes. It's the old, relentless Shadow again, doing what God made him to do.

Shady rises up on her hind legs to join me, toggling between whimpering and smelling. I watch her too for signs of recognition. I see none. And when Shadow comes back, he's not giving me anything either.

With my face turned away from Dan, I wipe off my eyes. "Negative," I say.

"Shoot," Dan replies.

"It don't mean he wasn't in here. Just that the scent ain't traceable."

"I can't do much with that, though."

I hand him Shady's leash and grab Shadow under the belly to bring him down. Whether he's showing off his limberness or not, I don't want him to take the shock of the jump.

We take a couple of minutes while Dan covers up the door. Part of me wonders how much clearing and covering up he did last time he was here, and whether the perp picked up on the disturbance. I won't tell him that, though. It's no use worrying about it, anyway.

As he's finishing up and picking up his backpack to put it back on, I notice Shadow. He's looking down trail, sniffing the air. Shady's doing the same, the two of them pointing like redundant arrowheads in case the humans need the reinforcement.

"We should probably walk a little further," I say.

Dan eyes the dogs. "You sure?"

"They are."

I still let him take Shady, but this time I take point with Shadow. He's honed in hard on something, I realize, not quite pulling on my leash, but as close to it as he comes. His ears are up, straight up, like he's getting a satellite beam or something more spiritual from up above to guide his way.

We don't walk far. We come up to it. I know we have when Shadow stops and will go no further.

Something sinks within me. I feel my thighs wobble for a moment before I tell myself if Shadow can do it, so can I. He's not cowering this time. He's staring it down, quiet and resolute like. So can I.

I raise my hand.

"What is it?" Dan asks.

"IED."

"What?"

"Bomb, under that pile of rocks."

Dan inches closer, and he points to it. Poking out from under one of the rocks I've seen it, too. A little bare foot. More than a foot, though, it's the bait.

Dan sprints back down trail and comes back riding his SUV. He's already called it in, tells me backup is on its way, will be here soon. The bomb squad, coming all the way from Denver, will take longer.

I'm sitting on a rock, about ten yards from the IED site, staring at it, both dogs at my side.

"You OK?" he asks me.

I think about his question, whether anyone can ever claim it, being OK, all the way OK.

"That boy in Estees," I say. "You're pretty convinced he wasn't related to this case. Why?"

"Ritual killing. Hate crime. Cross scratched on his forehead. You know, anti-Christian, they're thinking. Or sick Christian, who knows?"

"Or sweetening bait for this one."

"Huh?"

"I'll wager when you get this bomb dismantled and take them rocks off, you'll find a boy with a cross on his forehead."

"You say that like you've seen this before."

I look up at him. "I wrote this essay once. It's my best. So good I memorized it. Wanna hear it?"

He nods, and for the next few minutes I recite my PTSD story. No tears, no emotion, just a blank face and a monotone voice telling him about a little boy and his girl sister half a world away, how they were found, she tossed over the edge, him under a pile of rocks camouflaging an IED.

"When you talked to Brady last, did he mention or ask anything about the Estees killing?" I ask.

"No, he didn't."

"Well, let's see what he has to say now." I pick up my cellphone and dial up Lackland.

The bomb squad arrives shortly before sundown. They rush to set up field lights while the experts argue over what to do with the IED. As was the case back in Afghanistan, the quandary comes down to, do you, A, try to diffuse the bomb and risk loss of life in order to preserve the body and evidence, or B, blow up the whole thing, like you usually do when you find a bomb, and who cares about giving the family the body or whether there's any evidence that burns with it.

The argument went much along those lines back in Afghanistan when I found my first little boy. In that instance, they opted to diffuse the IED. When we uncovered the body underneath the rubble, someone theorized it probably wasn't a one-off occurrence. It looked too planned, too *serial*, some expert said. Which led me to wonder how many little boys were blown up before that one, destroying any evidence, just as the killer would want.

I wonder whether from somewhere in the dark he's watching us now, enjoying himself as we agonize over the choice he's given us. Takes one cruel mind to do that. How does one get that sick and twisted? I ask that, and hate it that I know the answer all too well.

Dan's side of the argument, the one about preserving evidence isn't going too well at the moment. That's when I notice them, both Shadow and Shady rising up, ears perked up, noses pointing to the south.

"You guys need help diffusing that IED," I say.

They all turn to me.

Some young too hot for himself guy shoots back, "And who should we call for that?"

I raise my hand, close my eyes, and say, "Listen."

Seconds later we can all hear it, the sound of an approaching helicopter.

"Help's here," I say, and keep my eyes closed to feel the wind pick up and swirl from the aircraft's downdraft.

Chapter 13

It's too late and not cost effective to find a motel, Dan insists by the time we leave the site at 3 AM in the morning. How about I go to his house, he suggests. Straight-up, he says, he's not going to try anything. Not that he would dare with Shadow and Shady in tow.

I don't see any sense in arguing against it. I've slept among plenty of guys in my time, in far closer quarters, and managed to keep my virginity until someone raped it out of me minutes before a blast tore off my legs. He's pleased when I accept.

At his house, Dan takes me to an upstairs guest room he has in an attic he converted into a loft. It works great, with plenty of room for the dogs. Home away from home, I dare to tease him before I take a quick shower and crash.

When I wake up, shortly before 9 AM, Shady's not with me. Shadow looks like he's been up for a while and ready to start his day. He and I go downstairs.

Dan greets me in the kitchen with Shady at his side. "I already took him out earlier."

"Looks like you've found your girlfriend."

"Hmm. Not so sure about that. She's not so good with following orders."

"She go out, too, I take it?"

"Mm-hmm." Dan gets up and goes to the stove where he has a premixed bowl of eggs and a pan at the ready. "Eggs and toast, OK?"

"Army grunt, remember? Yeah, more than OK. Thanks."

He does his thing, we eat our food mostly in silence, and as I'm taking the plates to the sink, we get back to business.

"Talked to Brady earlier."

I glance at the stove clock. It's now 9:40 AM. "How much earlier?"

"Bright. Oh-six hundred, like you guys say."

"I take it he didn't exactly wake you up."

"I called him."

"And he was very glad. Because he has a sudden interest in this case, don't he?"

"I got that vibe," Dan says.

"Bet you did." I turn to face him. "Last time you and Brady talked, seriously, did the manner in which that kid in Estees die come up?"

"I told you straight. No. But now I can see why you would think so, and more than that, I get why your boss becomes more interested in some missing kid on some Colorado mountain, when days before he just about deep-sixed the whole thing."

"Good. So you and I, we're starting to see the same picture."

"And a nasty one it is."

"Ain't it? War's hell. Makes people do nasty things. Flip out in all kinds of contorted ways."

He lets my words sit for a couple of seconds. "We got ID on the kid this morning. He's not the one we were tracking."

I sigh. "Jesus."

"Joseph and Mary."

"You Catholic?"

He shakes his head. "Just joshing. Listen—" He falters, like he's not keen on what he has to say. "I should take you and the dogs home. There really isn't much more to do here."

"That boy's still missing."

"What's your thinking?"

"We give it another go." I say that knowing the futility of it. The scent, whatever there was of it before I got pulled up into a helicopter and whisked to Lackland, is all gone by now. There's no use in me lingering here until the next body drops, or the next boy goes missing.

Dan waves his hand. "Look, I'm not the expert, but I've been reading and—"

"I know."

"So what are you saying?"

I should say the reason I want to stay is that I don't want to give up. I don't want to know I failed again. I don't want to admit all me and my dogs are good for is finding death and things that blow up. I could also admit I want to hang around him a little longer, but of all those other things, this one's the hardest to confess.

"Take me home," I say.

He nods, his eyes clouded with sadness. I'll look back at this moment as proof of how people fail most when they refuse to be honest with each other, to just say how they feel, what they believe, out of pride or for fear of rejection.

We get back to the ranch shortly before lunch. I offer Dan lunch, but he declines. Has to run back, he says, will grab something along the way. I don't know if that does it, or the little sleep, or the weight of the case, or the PTSD yanking me down by the hair. But I spend the rest of the afternoon lounging on the couch, getting up only to let the dogs go out, sitting on the porch to watch them, only to sink further as I sway on one of the rockers.

What am I doing now? What will I do next?

What do I have left to offer? What point is there to any of it? To me, actually. What's my point? Who on this world hangs on my existence? How would any of it be any different if I weren't here?

When I've sunk low enough, I stop asking questions. I sit there and wallow in the cold vacuum of answers too elusive to uncover or too painful to contemplate.

As if to stop me from taking the last step onto the landmine, Shadow comes lumbering up the steps and sits by me, staring at me with his one cloudy eye. Shady pounces onto the porch a moment later and does the same.

There they sit, the two answers God gives me right now. They're good for ten more years or so, but here they are if I can find nothing else. My reason to keep it together, to keep pushing, to keep food on my table and kibble in their bowls.

"You guys wanna do something?"

They both bark.

"Enough moping for one day, huh?"

Two more barks.

"Alright, let's go for a walk, then."

I slap my hands three times, the sign that this is all fun, no work. They receive that with energetic enthusiasm, and for now, I tell myself I should too.

"Or," I say. "How about a run? A fun run!"

They, especially Shady welcome that by circling me like tornadoes as I step into the house. In my bedroom they keep running around me, jumping on the bed—well that's all Shady—hopping up and down as I swap my clothes with running shorts and singlet. On my wrist I snap my GPS watch.

The running shoes go on last, and as I put them on, I articulate the mechanical ankle with my hand. It bends and twists, but gives increased resistance as it reaches its end points. I bend down to listen to any gears that may be spinning in there. I hear none, though both Shady and Shadow come over, ears full-on-up, noses up against it.

"That's right, my special feet," I tell them in

as girly a voice as my baritone throat can squeal out.

They go back to bouncing and prancing.

When we reach the front porch I loosen up a bit, but the stretching routines most people go through don't much apply to me. There are no calves to stretch, and try doing a quad stretch without lower legs. The hamstring stretch is about as pointless. Before I go all negative, I recount how most of my running injuries involved tight calves and the strain they cause on the Achilles tendon, plantar fasciitis, and chin splints. All gone now, thanks to an IED. As my preacher might say, all things working out for good right there. Hell of a way to keep that chin up, with emphasis on the hell.

Out into the late afternoon we go. We follow the same path out the back of the house. I roll out at an even, easy thirteen minute per mile pace most would call a fast walk. Shadow and Shady sprint out, into the grass, back onto the path, returning to me, circling behind me, back into the grass, and so on. Not the most efficient way to cover the distance, but it sure looks fun.

We pass the small hill on which Allison and I talked just as the angle of the sun turns light yellow to cast the dust and pollen rising from the grass in a golden haze. At this point I do what I do on most runs: think. Think about stuff that will take my mind off how much I hate running. Except this time, I go to thinking about why I hate running first. How much it hurts, how hot it makes me, how pointless it seems, without any particular goal in mind.

That right there is the main reason I hate running. That guy that died running the first marathon? He had a place to go and a message to deliver. In other words, there was a point to his misery—and death, I guess. People in Africa that run from village to village? That's how they get to work. Yeah, the point. We here in the west? Why in the world do we go running? Oh, to be fit. Because most of us sit for a living, and when we're not working inside a cardboard box, we're still sitting. Sitting in traffic. Sitting in front of the TV. Sitting in church. No wonder we're growing lard behinds. But is that reason to go for a run, to waste valuable time going nowhere in particular? Or maybe we need to eat a little less, watch a little less TV, do something other than punch a clock inside cube jail.

So far my run is producing very positive thoughts. But at least they differ from the mopey ones I was having back at the house.

At about a mile and half I reach the midpoint, and here I have a choice: double-back, or run around the long way for another two and half miles. I'm wanting to do the latter, but though he's still bounding about undeterred, I don't want to over-push Shadow, so back we go the way we came. By now I'm clocking a little under twelve minute pace and huffing plenty.

For a moment I entertain shooting up a prayer of thanksgiving for my ability to run. But the huffing keeps me from it, as does the pain in my thighs and lower back.

Dusk falls all around us, long shadows now giving way to darkness. As my thighs begin to burn, my thoughts turn once again to physical exercise. Now I dwell on its benefits. You know, all that claptrap you hear about endorphins and health benefits. I'd like to take one of them experts through one of my first PT sessions, hell, any PT session by someone trying to learn how to walk again on foreign objects that God didn't design. Yeah, go through that excruciation, and see if it don't cure you of all misconceptions about the benefits of physical exertion.

The ache in my thighs and back reminds me of that, the physical pain of trying to control something foreign, of learning to balance yourself on something that won't move when your nerves want it to. But at least this pain bears no connection with the frustration and embarrassment of failure. I'm upright now, moving, pain and all, but not falling, not having to rely on someone or some contraption or padding below to keep me from hitting a hard floor.

Just as I round the small hill to finish out the last home stretch, Shadow leaps from the tall grass holding a thick piece of branch in his teeth.

Only my desire to finish out the run without interruption keeps me going. But seeing him trotting alongside me, looking up with that stick in his mouth threatens to turn me into mush.

I avert my eyes and look ahead.

How long has it been since we last played fetch? He pretty much gave up on thinking it fun at around the one year mark. Even though I tried to play with him during his free time, he would mostly chase the stick, sniff it, and leave it. I remember thinking I could correct him, but with all the work he did, with how he got the serious stuff right, I never had the heart for it. I also realized he more or less stopped playing as soon as we were deployed and after he saw his first action. Like all of us did. We stopped being boys and girls then forever, and we got hard inside. No more fetching sticks. Just real, bloody, shattered life.

But whatever happened then, he's still clamping down on that thick thing when we reach the front of the house. Out of breath, I go down to his level to look him in that one eye. I grab that stick out of his mouth and I hurl it.

It doesn't go far, as I didn't stand right to throw it, so he fetches it quick and brings it back. He's really doing this, ain't he?

I take the proper throwing stance this time, and the stick goes flying in a long arc. Shadow takes after it with agility I haven't yet seen from him. Like a pup. Like that hip is fully healed. I'm about to dwell on that, his hip, when I see Shady. She's panting heavily, sitting on the porch, looking at us. This surprises me because she's the kind to get into the mix and rile things up by chasing and grabbing for the stick. The way she looks back at me is surprising, too, like she's saying, "That's alright, you two can have your moment."

By then Shadow is back on me, nudging the stick into my hand. I throw it again, and off he goes. As he comes back, I go down to his level again and stretch out my arms, like a little girl welcoming back her cub.

When he reaches me this time, he drops the stick a couple of feet away from me and gets all the way into me before he sits. I wrap my arms around his neck and realize: I'm squatting. Yeah, I'm down for a full squat. How did that happen, I start to ask, when something else takes over me, and I start crying.

Shadow whimpers once. Behind me I feel Shady's breath on my neck. She lets out one long whistling whine. It pierces through me. It undoes me. I am not crying anymore. I am gushing. I am holding onto Shadow, and behind me Shady secures me with her nose. They let me be. They let me melt into their fur. And I weep, finally falling onto my butt and drawing my knees into my chest while they surround me.

I don't know how long I stay there, but when I come to, only the timer-enabled light form the porch breaks the otherwise pitch black around us.

"Hey, you know what?" I tell them, my face still a wet mess. "How about throwing something real heavy?"

They both bark. I get up, with surprising ease, considering my burned out thighs, and I go to the garage. From a small fridge I take out a bottle of water and drain it in one go. Then I uncover a wheelbarrow. I run my hand along the top shot put shells it holds, feeling the rust of them scratch against my hand. I pat down the chalk bag and decide there's enough in there for a session. I pick up the wrist strap and put it on.

With Shady and Shadow at either side of me, I lift and roll out the wheelbarrow. I reach the far end of the front yard where I usually do this, though at the moment I can't clock the last time I—aspiring Olympian if my agent-run Twitter feed tells the truth—ran through these motions. Too much time shouldn't have passed, I assure myself, judging from the still visible faint circle which I now retrace and carve with my foot.

Having seen me do this before, Shady knows where to sit: by the wheelbarrow, away from the direction the crazy big woman is hurling them heavy balls. Shadow looks around and decides to join her.

I smile at them, and then my eyes let go again. My high school and college days come rushing back. I see myself whole again, tossing shots from the spring of two strong legs. Enough of that, I tell myself as I wipe my face. With a sniffle, I reach into the wheelbarrow, slap some chalk on my hands, and grab the first ball. I bring it to my shoulder and feel the weight of it. God, that's heavy. Like it wants to crush me. Like it wants to drill me into the ground.

That's when my eyes threaten to unfurl again, but I don't let them. I shut them tight and I clench my teeth. No, this first ball, this one is for that first little boy. I assume the position, balance out with my left arm, breathe in, go into the rotation, and I let it out with a scream.

My eyes still want to let go, but no, they will not. I grab the second ball, go back to my circle, set up again. This one's for those shot-up parents and their teenage boy. Another rotation, another scream into the night, and the ball streams into the light cast by the front porch.

I'm not caring about distance. I'm not taking note of where they fall, just that they fly out of my hand, so I go for number three. This one's for the rape, for those three bastards that grinned and grunted through it. Then the fourth, for my legs, for the pain of losing them, for the further disfigurement to an already undesirable body.

I scream. I let it go, from my dark corner of the yard into the light it goes.

Shady lets out a short howl.

Then there's that fifth one. The one for the kids on that Afghan mountain, and the kids here in Colorado I could not get to. I throw it and I scream. And Shady howls with me.

I go for number six. What will this one stand for? I see Shadow starting back at me. Calm, unfazed, his black coat folding into the night. Do it girl, you know what to do. From the dark into the light. Throw it girl, he's telling me with that one foggy eye that is nothing but a dark hole now.

Yeah, this one's for you, Shadow. Because you're a hero, more noble and unselfish than all of us put together. This is for you, for the way you also came back mangled, and I scream loudest when I hurl it for you. And I crash down as it leaves my hand, and I cry.

I get up. There's more. I gotta throw at least one more. So I reach for it, not knowing what it stands for. I draw it to my shoulder all the same, and I stretch out my left arm. I breathe in, I hold it, and I hop, turn and let it go. I watch it fly and catch the light. At that moment I know what it represents: my fear, my self-loathing, the way I've been beating myself up for all that's happened to me when there's more, so much more, and I should just say thank you that I can face it, even if in pain, even if I have to swim through dark streams and battle devious demons along the way.

I go down on one knee, then the other, and I cry. Shadow and Shady surround me again with their coats. Here I am, what's left of me, still in the dark, crumbled inside it, but straining for the light.

I claw my way there, on all fours, screaming, crying out. Next to me Shady bark-howls, and Shadow whines softly. If no one else understands my anguish, they do, not because I tell them about it, but because they get me in that place that requires no words or explanations.

Almost there, at the corner edge of the porch, Shadow growls, then barks with recognition. I place one hand on the wooden deck and use it to bring myself up to a standing position.

There I see her, in the light, in front of a Jeep. She's dressed in her BDUs, wearing her cover. She stands at attention and salutes.

"Lieutenant Cassandra Godinez reporting for duty, ma'am."

Chapter 14

"What the hell do you think you're doing here, Lieutenant, Captain Select, or whatever you are?"

"I'm here on orders ma'am."

"Whose orders?"

"I think you know that already, ma'am."

"OK, what orders?"

"To assist you in whatever you need."

I walk up to her. My face and eyes remain a soggy mess, but I'm betting the expression I'm flashing her makes the other part the least of her concerns. I get right up against her. I glare down on her, inches from her face.

"Do I look like I need a babysitter, Lieutenant?"

With her neck craning back, she weighs her answer for a moment. "Respectfully, I rather not say, ma'am."

"And why's that?"

"Manners."

I step back and let out a bitter chuckle. "Manners. Now that's a fine answer. Shouldn't we wish we had more soldiers with *manners*."

Godinez clenches her jaw.

"I bet you're proud you saw that whole show. Now you get to report back something messy-juicy. Make sure to tell them it's part of my therapy, much better than that regurgitation crap they have me do down in Lackland."

"There's no shame in it, ma'am."

"Shame in what?"

"In wrestling with it."

"How sweet of you, not perturbed by spying on a fellow soldier when she's crying."

She takes a moment before saying, "Tears and crying are good. My Grandmother says tears and crying, that's how springs of hope bust through."

My momentum urges me to carry on forward with another cynical retort. But something stops me. Maybe it's the way she said that and the way those words ripple through me. Maybe it's exhaustion, because in an instant, I feel tired, like I need to sit down, so I do, on the edge of the porch. Shady comes over, and I scratch behind her ears.

"Your Granma sounds like a woman of faith," I say.

"She is. And a poet. That line is from a poem she wrote."

I look up at Godinez again. My voice turns raspy. "I'd like to read it sometime."

"I can get you a copy." She takes out her cellphone. "I have it here—"

I wave her off. "Great, great. Not right now. But thank you." I take two long breaths. "You caught me at a hell of a time."

"Aren't they all?"

"Yeah, maybe." I smile at her, and I realize she's beginning to get under my skin, the good way. "It's dinner time, Lieutenant. Have any plans for that?"

"Not really, ma'am." The way she says that makes me suppose she's been watching me all day on nothing but water and granola bars.

"So what you're saying is you drove all the way up here, hoping to self-invite yourself to dinner."

"No, ma'am. I'm not saying that at all."

I take another deep breath and stand up. "Godinez, honey. Let me give you a helpful tip. If you want to have any chance of me liking you, don't call me ma'am. I'm already feeling washed out enough as it is. Call me by my rank, or call me Jane."

"Thank you, Major—"

"On second thought, let's leave it at Jane."

"OK, and you can call me Cassandra, m— Jane."

"Swell. You like spaghetti, of the left-over variety, *Cassandra*?"

Her voice turns cheery. "Sure. I eat anything."

I climb up the steps as I say, "I'm sure you

do."

Cassandra being Hispanic and telling me her grandmother was a woman of faith, I play the law of averages and assume she's Catholic. Wrong. It turns out she's more conservative evangelical than I am supposed to be, enough so that she blushes—yes, blushes through her smooth olive skin—when I pop a cork and offer her a glass of red wine.

By unstated mutual agreement, we let our simple dinner time slide by with everyday banter about education (she has a master's in Computer Science), career, tours of duty (3 for her, all Afghanistan; 4 for me, split evenly between Iraq and Afghanistan), family history, future plans, and so on.

She has seconds of the spaghetti, big kudos for me, I guess, or she hasn't eaten since sunup, is more likely. I watch her over the rim of my wine glass, let her get near the end of that second helping.

"So how does this work, you and me?" I ask.

"You call, I come."

"Sounds simple enough. I take it you have a closer home base now."

"Yup. Got reassigned to Warren."

She means Francis E. Warren Air Force Base, just up the I-25 in Wyoming, about 45 minutes way. Not a bad commute, all things considered.

"That's gotta be a bummer for you. Away from the training center and all."

"You'd be surprised." She almost winks at me as she twirls the last spoonful of spaghetti into her mouth.

"I'd be surprised you're sick of dogs? I'd be surprised you don't want to go on another deployment? Or I'd be surprised there's some interesting stuff at Warren to keep your juices flowing?"

"A little of all that, but a full discussion would need another venue."

"Oh, cool stuff," I say. "Stuff that no one's supposed to know about and whispers boom in the night."

She smiles. "We should be careful."

"Oh, yes. We best be just that." I take a swallow from my glass, the last swallow of my second glass, and I'm thinking I should call it quits there. But given her earlier blushing and all, I can't resist taking a look at her face as I pour one more glass which I promise myself is just there for looks.

"OK," I say, now swirling the wine in the glass. "So you're 45 minutes away. I guess if I need something I should allow at least that much lead time."

Godinez smiles. The way her dark brown eyes twinkle I'm guessing she's coming back with something interesting and is trying to figure out how best to voice it.

"Or we could make other arrangements," she says.

"Oh, we could, could we? Anything special in mind?"

She grins. "I could be closer."

"How close do you have in mind?"

"I think you know."

"Here, my house. It's fresh enough of you to invite yourself over for dinner. But what now? I'm supposed to go make my guestroom ready for you?"

"Just something to think about. It would simplify things."

"And what's the point of this, Cassandra, dear? You bring me some more dogs, we train 'em here, and I mentor you, like Brady wants? Show you how to make warrior dogs?"

"That wouldn't happen here, though having my dog local would be nice."

"So no training here. Then why the roommate bit?"

She steals a glance at Shadow before turning back to me. "I think you know that, too."

"Do I? How exactly am I supposed to know? No one told me."

"But you know."

"And you know I know." I feel a heat rising up in my chest. "Just how long have you been watching me?"

"I'm not at liberty to say, but you can guess."

Yeah, I can guess alright. And I'm guessing they know all about Allison and me snooping into Shadow via MRI. Maybe they even anticipated and planned for our eventual discovery. It would stand to reason, wouldn't it? My friend the Vet doctor wanting to look into Shadow's health to better understand the extent of his injuries? Sure it would.

I say, "So you've come to protect Uncle Sam's asset."

"Assets, plural."

I lean back in my chair. "Excuse me. Plural." I point at Shadow. "So him." I point at me. "And yours truly?"

"I think we should stop there and talk this out in a different venue."

"How exactly am I an asset?" I slap my thighs. "Did someone miss a couple of pages in the report, the ones that spell out the amputations, plural?"

She looks down, as if she could see my sawed off legs through the table. "Again, a full discussion requires a different venue."

"That's just the thing, Casandra. I don't talk in different venues. I've been read out. I'm just a lowly regular citizen doing reservist duty every six weeks."

"That runs contrary to my understanding on the matter, ma'am. Excuse me, Jane."

I start to object. I almost tell her I signed a stack of papers when I got debriefed. Then I recall. I did it on a gurney they rolled in to some vault—the right *venue*—where we could speak freely. Except we didn't speak much, or if we did, hell if I remember. I was so doped up, I really don't much recall what I signed. I could have committed to donate all seven of my kidneys, for all I know.

"So I'm still in."

"Yes, ma'am."

"In some project we can't talk about, but you're here to protect."

"Correct."

"A project that involves him and me."

"Affirmative."

"OK, then. Did you at least bring a toothbrush?"

"Yes, ma'am."

"Alright. I guess I should go off and make your bed."

"That's not necessary. I can take care of it myself, ma'am."

I look into her bright eyes, and I can't tell whether I see glee or mocking there. "Yeah, I bet you can do that and much more," I reply. "And please, really, drop the ma'am calling."

I sit there, now staring at my glass of wine, wondering how much of the *rumor* I told Allison about was no rumor at all, but rather something my tangled psyche did not quite grasp as someone explained it to me. I take the glass, and I down it in three clumsy swallows.

Chapter 15

Morning comes to the rhythmic pounding of a hundred needles in my head. It brings also the reminder that while I once stood at 6′ 1″, my true anatomical height diminished nearly one third thanks to an IED and the hacksaw that followed it. That leaves me with less blood into which I can pour alcohol, and them three red glasses last night now scream the wisdom of a clean and sober life.

Morning also comes with the smell of brewing coffee and a hint of Vanilla mixed in. In the kitchen I find Cassandra with her nose above her cup, and a smiling offer to pour me one of my own. I wave her off. She shrugs me off with a smile, though by the look in her eye, she's picked up the trail on my hangover.

She chooses to ignore my state of disrepair, saying instead something about an explosion with boulders.

"Come by me again?" I ask as I finish pouring my cup.

"I was watching the news early. There was an explosion down in Boulder, around that same park where they found that other boy under the pile of rocks."

She leaves it there, but I know that she knows the boy was found with an IED on him as well. For some reason she's chosen to leave that unsaid, and I don't push her on it.

I find my cell on the counter, where I left it, tethered to its charger. Before I dial Dan's number, I see he sent me a text. "Come down if you can. Need to talk. F2F."

Those last three letters tell plainly of his intentions. I could call him, but he doesn't want to talk on the phone. He'd rather handle whatever information he wants to discuss face to face.

Godinez says, "I'll drive." She looks me up and down. "I recommend you wash up. I can put some breakfast together, to go if you prefer."

I look *her* up and down. "Sure. Make it burritos."

As I turn to go to the bathroom she replies, "I'll take that as a compliment and a vote of confidence in my cooking abilities."

"Yeah, that's about right."

"Do I have to make tortillas from scratch?"

"Check the garage fridge. I got a package out there. Sorry if you don't fancy the multi-grain kind."

I go in the bathroom and do my thing in the tub. I call it my sitting bull bath. Count that as something else they rip from you when your legs go away: the ability to stand under a shower. Sure, I could have a pair of plastic prosthetics. But I don't. For reasons I now understand a tad clearer, both of my sets of legs have metal in them, and God knows what other manner of mechanics and electronics. Good ol'

H_2O and them don't mix—I remember that much from the first orientation session, its admonitions making more sense in light of recent revelations.

All the same, I've gotten pretty good at this. I feel like an elephant seal doing it, but I roll in dry, roll out wet onto a towel I leave on the floor, dry myself with a second one I leave on the closed toilet seat. In between, soaping up and rinsing off takes, you guessed it, less time given the reduction in bodily surface area. Mark that as one more slash on the plus column for how all things work out for the good.

Having made myself presentable, I add three aspirin gels to the mix, and by the time I return to the kitchen even Cassandra's expression must acknowledge I stand a heck of a lot more ready for the day than I was twenty minutes ago.

She's been busy, too. I catch her wrapping up the second of two burritos in aluminum foil. Next to them on the counter I see two of my running water bottles filled with ice and orange juice.

"We should be good to go," Cassandra says. "Car's packed with gear and supplies. Dogs fed and brushed." She stops to smile at me. "And you look pretty cleared hot yourself."

"Careful now, Lieutenant. That might sound too close to sexual harassment right there."

"I won't tell if you don't ask." She flashes me a wink.

I look her up and down again, wondering if I really have her all sorted out. In the end, I decide to simply wink back.

Cassandra not so much offers as informs me she'll do the driving. I don't balk. As I'd hoped, we take my 4Runner, the bigger, though not necessarily more comfortable of our two vehicles. By the time we reach I-25, I've eaten half my burrito. She's laced it with bacon and diced tomatoes, and I'm savoring it, thinking having her around ain't such a bad deal.

When I'm done with it, I text Dan with our current location. He texts me back to give me the meet location: same spot where we checked out that camouflaged Bronco, right around where we found that other boy's boulder-piled grave. He tells me I'll know right where it is. I can't miss it, he assures me.

We arrive there a few minutes south of 1100, and he's right. It's plain as day. I don't know what I see first, the black gash and avalanche on the mountain side, or the TV crews, but doubt has no foothold here.

"Don't drive in all the way," I tell Cassandra. "I'll walk it."

"You sure you don't want me with you?"

"Nah, stay back with the dogs. Last thing I need right now is TV crews accosting me."

She gets it. We shouldn't leave the dogs in the SUV, and we can't walk them over there. My celebrity carries its liabilities.

Before I walk into the circus, I try to spot Dan. I can't, and I don't want to get in there without knowing exactly where he is. I dial his number. It goes to voice mail.

With Godinez at my side, I say, "Hey, Dan. Jane. I'm here. Where are you? Don't want to cause a scene."

At the moment I hang up, I spot it. The scene. I pull out my binoculars, and sure enough, I see Dan, in the middle of a throng of reporters, cameras in his face, boom microphones hanging overhead.

"Is that him?" Godinez asks.

"Yeah."

"Seems pretty stuck."

I think about options for a moment. "Wanna hear an idea on how to get him unstuck?"

"Sure."

I tell her we're walking in with the dogs after all and instruct her on what to do once we get there. She hesitates for a moment before smiling to give me a thumbs-up, and dive, dive, dive, in we go.

Sure enough, the reporters spot me. Or, to keep my ego in check, they spot two very large dogs, one of them pretty scary, and then the big gal with them. The news crews have either had enough of Dan, or they see a huge ratings bump in their future because in unison they swarm toward me.

"Jane McMurtry!" the first one's yelling like I just won the Super Bowl. "What can you tell us about your involvement in this case?"

We stop, I let the cameras form in a nice semicircle, boom mics and all, then I say, "I'm sorry, but I'm not at liberty to discuss details of how I've assisted in this case. However, Lieutenant Cassandra Godinez, herself an expert in this field, will be able to field general questions about how these two amazing animals perform this type of work."

Before the effects of that stun grenade dissipate, I run off. A few yards off, I wave to Dan, who follows me. We cross the yellow tape, and stop just inside it to talk.

Dan's thanking me for rescuing him, but I'm not really listening. I'm looking up at the black gash in the near vertical boulder field.

"What in darnation happened here?"

He looks around to make sure we're far away from prying ears. "Brady did it."

"Huh?"

"I spotted him, by chance, as I was coming

back to re-check that Bronco. Saw him climb up there, dig around the boulders, get something out. I should have stopped him then."

"Why didn't you?"

"I had no idea what he was doing. I wanted to see enough to have enough. You, know, evidence to hold him. So I watch him climb up, higher up, and before I realize it, he picks up a boulder and drops it down on the grave before taking cover."

"You mean?"

"Blew up the whole thing."

I swallow. I can't take the measure of that. I don't know if it's the residue hangover, or the sense something's way off, but my world has come off its hinges.

Dan helps me steady myself. "You OK?"

"Another boy that had gone missing?"

"Yeah. Less than a day."

I bring one hand to my mouth. "This is jacked up!"

"I talked to him. At gun point."

"Jesus, Dan. Those parents won't have a little

boy to bury. Won't even know that was him!"

"Actually, Brady thought of that." Dan takes out his phone. "When he was digging around the boulders, this is what he was after." He shows me a picture of a small shoe. Inside it, under the flap, the boy's name is inscribed. "Andy."

"Did he say why he did it?" I ask.

"Couldn't really get a straight answer out of him. Something about not wanting to risk his unit again, that he'd lost too many good men and women to IEDs. I told him that sounded like BS. He said there was no point in preserving evidence. That he'd *handled it*. When I pressed him on that, he said that he'd personally seen to it. That the possibility of another one of these murders is one hundred percent gone."

"You have him in custody?"

"Kind of."

"Meaning?"

"He asked me to contact you before I formally arrested him. Or before I did anything irreversible, is the way he put it. Said he wanted to talk to you. So I'm going on a limb here, Jane. For you."

"Where is he?"

"Cuffed in the back of my Tahoe. Under a tarp with lots of water and an ice cooler."

"I can't believe this," I say.

"Just say the word, and I take the crazy Colonel in."

"There's more to this, Dan. Let me talk to him. Get to the bottom of it."

"OK, if that's what you want. One condition, though. I'm there when you talk to him."

I think about that, about what rat holes I'm about to dive into, and whether Brady will open them unless he and I talk one on one. I'm also sensing something, smelling it like Shadow from far away. Whatever Brady wants to tell me ties this case to me, and not just me tracking boys in Afghanistan. The hole goes deeper than that. I have no evidence, yet I know it. Do I want Dan to hear that? Am I ready to let him all the way inside my darkest, starkest rat holes?

I look over at Godinez and see her doing the

Public Affairs thing. She seems to be enjoying it and handling those reporters with a deft touch. I consider her involvement in all this for a second. How much does she know? How far in with Brady has she gotten? Time will tell, I suppose.

I don't know why or how, but I make the call with clarity and zero doubt. "Set it up. Text me where to show up."

Chapter 16

Dan arranges the meet in a warehouse on the outskirts of town. He texts me that Brady will be chained up when I get there, and that he, Dan, will meet me outside. Now for the tricky part on my end. How do I get Cassandra to drive me there, not come in with me, and not get a whiff that her boss is in custody?

I feel her out on the way there. If I'm as good a reader of people as I am of dogs, I don't get the sense that she and Brady have had contact over the past couple of days. Back at the ranch, she also seemed somewhat taken aback by the explosion as reported in the news. I take all that to add up to, no, she's not in the know, at least not all the way in. But I still need to make sure I keep her at a safe distance.

When we drive up, I tell her, "I'm taking both dogs. The police want only me in there. You know how they get about contamination of crime scenes and all that."

She eyes Dan's Tahoe, the only police vehicle in sight. "Doesn't seem like much of a crime scene."

"Very low key, highly sensitive. Don't want to let the perp know we've gotten this close." I tap her on the forearm. "Can I trust you with this?"

"Yeah, of course."

"Do you have a piece on you?"

She reaches under the seat and takes out a Beretta 9 mm.

"Good. Chamber a round for me, OK? Eyes wide open."

Her eyes open a tad wider, and I think I got her convinced.

"Please, Cassandra. This dude is nasty, OK? Be careful. See anything, call me on my cell on the double."

"Alright. I got it," she says with a bit of annoyance, and I know I've pushed my little acting job far enough.

With Shady and Shadow on leash, I walk into the warehouse through a door labeled #5 in big white graffiti letters, as Dan described it in his text. A few steps in, I meet Dan.

I raise my hand, look back in the direction of my 4Runner. Cassandra's still in there.

I turn Shady to face the door, tell her to sit, and give her the watch command.

"OK, let's go," I whisper, and Shadow and I follow Dan up a set of metal stairs.

At the top I stop again to repeat what I did down below. Shadow looks up at me, and in the dark, I can't see his eye. I repeat the command, and he sits at attention, his snout pointed straight down those stairs.

"This is the only way in, right?" I ask Dan as we walk down a corridor.

"To this floor, yes."

"Good. If my buddy decides to join the party, I have at least two warning bells going off." I grab Dan by the arm. "Before we go in there," I whisper, "just know that I'm not going to do anything stupid, OK? Let me lead the chat with Brady, and no matter what I do, don't stop me. OK?"

"What are you going to do?"

"Impress him." We lock eyes, here in the faint yellow light of this hallway, and as I keep squeezing his arm, I hope he'll let me do what I need to do. "Trust me."

"OK."

"And you're going to hear some nasty things. Some probably about me. If you don't want to know, this is your chance to bow out."

He takes a little longer this time before he repeats, "OK."

"That the door?" I ask him. When he nods, I go in first. I take in the room in one quick sweep: a machine shop, what remains of it, rusted pieces of machinery strewn all about.

"Jane," Brady says with a grin-smile that vanishes when he sees Dan step in behind me. "He can't be here."

"Oh, yes, he can," I say like I'm chanting a political campaign slogan.

He sits a bit straighter in his stool, as if to signify his defiance. His right wrist is chained to a dusty lathe, which in turn is bolted to a metal top table.

He says, "Then we won't be able to have a full discussion. Not here."

"Oh, yes, we can," I say in the same tone. I reach to the small of my back and my hand comes out with my handgun. For effect, I chamber a round. Still for effect, with finger off the trigger I wave the gun at nothing in particular. "We are most definitely going to have a full and flowing discussion, *sir*."

"Jane, come off it. What do you think you're doing here?"

"You've read my psych reports. Who the hell knows what I'm doing at any given time!" Again, with finger off the trigger, on the barrel this time, I wave the gun at my head, twirl it in the general area of my right ear.

"*Estoy muy loca*," I say in my best Spanish

accent. "Like I'm sure that hot Mexican chili you sent my way's been reporting. Why just last night I was howling at the moon. Didn't she tell you?"

"Jane, please, it's not like that."

"Well, here's your chance, Colonel. Tell me just how it is."

He eyes Dan. I pull a stool and sit about ten feet from Brady. I drop the gun on the table, and it makes a deep metallic thump.

"I've done all this for you, Jane." His voice has dropped a notch in volume, and a couple more in pitch. "Because I know I failed you when it counted, and this is how I made it right. And I did. I made it right all the way."

"Sounds mighty good, but I'm not getting the details."

I see his thick neck muscles ripple as he swallows. "The deputy has my phone. Some pictures in there will show what I mean."

"It's password locked," Dan says as he steps up to hand me Brady's phone.

Brady shoots me a heavy stare. "Code is,

Shadow dash number seven dash Jane," he says.

My hand is shaking as I hold the phone. I hesitate to type. All this time, for as long as he's had this phone, he's had this code on it. Why? To remind himself? To remember me and Shadow, and what we had together?

I collect myself and type the code, Shadow-7-Jane.

"First three pictures, look familiar?" Brady asks.

My eyes blur with tears, but yeah, I recognize them. The three guys that raped me.

"We don't have to keep going," Brady says.

I keep scrolling. Now I see three more pictures. Bloody pictures. I have to review them one more time before I confirm: it's the same three faces, this time disfigured, each with a single bullet hole above the bridge of the nose.

"They're gone," Brady says. "Forever. Never to hurt you or anyone else again."

"You did this?" I ask.

"And no one else."

"So now, to destruction of a crime scene and

interfering with a crime investigation, we can add murder," Dan says. "In triplicate, no less."

Brady looks up at him. "You were never going to get those guys. As for murder in triplicate, while three photos on my phone may seem like tremendous evidence, you'll have one hell of a time proving I did it. Good luck. Especially finding the bodies, which I promise you no longer exist."

Brady looks back at me. "We should stop now, Jane. You get it. No need to go further."

"Why did you blow up that little boy, Brady? Why not let his parents bury him?"

He looks back at Dan before he returns his gaze to me. "They stashed a picture of you with the boy. Their last cruel joke. I know how close to the edge you've been. I didn't want you all over the news, possibly pulled into a court of law to relive what they did to you."

"Nah, I ain't buying that, Brady. There's more to it, ain't there?"

"Please, Jane. I did it for you."

"You did it for you, you sanctimonious

bastard. You did it for your little project, because my over-exposure would blow the whole thing." I stop there, because even this doesn't add up in total. I'm missing a variable somewhere, and somehow I land upon it.

"Oh, but wait," I press on. "There's more. You're going to love this, Dan. It explains why I got pulled off that mountain. Because those bastards wanted *me* to find the kid. They wanted *me* to be standing there in front of the cameras when they pulled not only my picture out of the grave, but something else. A folder detailing Brady's precious little program, perhaps?"

Brady goes to stand up, but his chain is too short. "Please, Jane. Think of the damage this will do to the country, to the warfighter. Stop right there. Go no further."

"You might have to give that command in Dutch or German, Brady, because this bitch ain't fetching for you no more."

"I'm a little lost," Dan says.

"Six months ago, in Louisville," I say. "In two hours me and Shady found that missing girl and boy, remember? The police went on and on about me, I got all famous on the Internet, them saying how they would always call me for anything in the Colorado area. How I could always consult for them. These guys got wind of that, and they built this whole missing person scenario knowing I'd get called in. Me and my special legs."

"Please Jane," Brady says again, though now I'm hearing resignation in his voice.

"I can't take this anymore," I say. I slide the safety on, and stick the gun in the back of my pants. "He's all yours, Dan. Your call."

I stomp out of the room and get halfway down the hallway before Dan catches up with me.

"Hey, hold up," he says as he grabs me by the arm. He turns me around and holds me by both shoulders. "I need to know a little more here."

"He's right, Dan. If he goes down, it'll give those bastards what they wanted. Maybe even louder and more amplified than they intended.

My rape all over the news, the way the Marines concealed it, which they won't care about, now that they're good and dead, Brady's program—"

"OK, OK. I get all the other stuff. But this program you keep talking about... What's it about? Something secret?"

"It's secret, yes. I could go to jail for spilling it. You could, too."

"But there's something more."

"Yeah. It helps soldiers that come back injured." I swallow. "Did you ever wonder how I got around so well up those steep, rocky trails, Dan?"

He can't help it. He looks down. To his credit, he looks back up, right away, right into my eyes. "What do you want me to do?"

"I can't make this call, Dan. You're the law here. I'm not. I'm just a tracker."

He squeezes my shoulders. "Like hell you are. You're not just a tracker to me. We're making this call together."

"You mean I tell you what I want, and you do it. That's not how it's going to play either,

Dan. You have to feel right about this. You're not going to pin this on me, hold it over me."

"Fair. But don't pin it on me either."

"Well, here's the thing, big boy. You *are* the law here. I'm not. It is *your* call."

He brings his head down until our foreheads touch. "That's where you're wrong, Jane," he whispers. "I am the law, but I'm much more than that. And you're the reason for that much more."

Chapter 17

Cassandra convinces me to find a local motel, and though I rather make the drive home, we check into one at around 2 AM. Dan has said he may need us back first thing in the morning, though he doesn't say why. I suppose in spite of my desire to get back to my own bed, this works out best.

We get a room with two twin beds and enough space between them to fit Shadow's bed while Shady takes up residence on the bathroom rug.

"Cozy," Cassandra says.

"And a heck of a lot more room than we'd have you know where."

"Word," she replies. "Count our blessings."

She goes to bed counting her blessings, I suppose, and that puts her down to sleep in less than a minute. Me? I count many things, none of them conducive to pleasant dreams. Rest comes to me in shallow, short bursts, each broken by some memory of Iraq or Afghanistan, when I didn't have many blessings to count. At around 3:30 in the morning, I estimate, I fall asleep, only to come up startled by the ringing of our room's phone. By now it's 4:45 AM.

Cassandra gets to it first. Rubbing her eyes, she says, "OK, let me get something to write with." On the nightstand she finds pen and paper and jots something down that looks like an address.

She hangs up. "Dan." She yawns and waves the sheet of paper. "Wants us at this address as quick as we can get there."

"What is it?"

"Missing kid." She pauses "Another boy."

My stomach churns at the thought. But I don't think. I execute, and that means first of all, put on them fancy legs. Ten minutes later, after getting dressed and washing our faces, in that order, we're out the door.

On the way we feed the dogs some biscuits, and Cassandra and I munch down granola bars. It takes us about twenty minutes to arrive at a mobile home park. Sunlight is beginning to hint at its arrival on a deep blue eastern sky. Rising hills and fields butt against the edge of the last row of mobile homes, and in the distance, the Rockies rise against a black western sky.

"News van," Cassandra points out. "INN," she adds, reading the insignia of newly minted Independent News Network. Cassandra mutters something under her breath that sounds like a curse. I give her a quizzical look, and she says, "Bridget Suarez. Reporter. Stay clear of her."

Two cameras point at us, each of their red lights on to let us know, yes, as a matter of fact, they're recording our arrival. Fortunately a wall of law enforcement vehicles and officers separate us from them. Though Suarez shouts a question at us, we got enough room between us to ignore it without seeming overly rude.

Dan meets us at the entrance into the mobile home park.

"What do we have?" I ask.

"Boy went missing sometime in the middle of the night. Climbed out or was taken through a window."

"Connected?"

Something about the way I say that or the expression on my face makes him step up and whisper. "I'm not sure. My soft money is on, no, but we need to check it out." He leans a little closer, enough to make me uncomfortable. "They have another canine team here. Police. Not too happy you got called in. Then again, they're finding jack."

Though I'm tempted to ask what problem the other team has encountered, I don't. Best to approach the scene with a fresh perspective, unbiased by what the other guy has gotten stuck on, even if in some situations that ends up wasting time from repeating steps and even going down already explored side tracks that lead to dead ends.

Sure enough, as we approach a police huddle, I spot the K-9 handler, none too happy to be up this early, and less enthused to see me and my two dogs. I hesitate for a moment before I hand Shadow's leash to Cassandra. Keeping Shady and Shadow together, she stays a few steps away while I introduce myself to my civilian counterpart.

He immediately launches into his own version of what's going on. I nod, as if I'm listening, while through my left ear I spy on the conversation among top brass and Dan Murphy. It's hard to focus, with this guy going a mile a minute in front of me, but I gather the missing kid, a ten year old boy, took off on his own after an argument with his parents. As reported by the mom, the boy told his dad he wanted to go missing like those other boys.

That diminishes my apprehension. As we drove here, and now as I stand ready to give chase, I've asked myself whether I'm ready for another one of these. Can I handle another boy under a pile of rocks? Should I go on pretending seeing another one won't rip me up inside?

I don't have much time for introspection. By now the lead officer's on me, waving a teddy bear.

A teddy bear, I think, fighting to unfreeze myself and to push down memories of another teddy bear on a faraway land.

"Same one the other K-9 sniffed?" I manage to ask.

"Yeah. If you want something else we can get it, but the parents say he sleeps with it every night."

"Sleeps with it but left it behind," I hear myself say, not quite knowing what point I want to make with those words, but seeing in the frowns and looks the cops exchange they think I just made a crucial, previously neglected point.

"Care to elaborate on that?" Dan asks.

"Just that I would expect the boy to take it with him." I take the toy and go over to my dogs. "But I'm just the tracker. I'll leave the observations and theories to you all and go about my trackin'."

Both Shady and Shadow, eager for the work, latch on to the scent at once. One of the officers takes me to the window where the boy allegedly climbed through.

"He wasn't here," I say at once.

"Our guy couldn't find any indication here either."

Of course, he didn't, because that boy didn't climb out of no window. I'm also wondering whether at age ten he's long grown out of the sleeping with teddy bears phase. I don't say that, though. Instead I ask to go in the house.

Some discussion follows about a search warrant vs. parents that shouldn't hesitate to give us full access and cooperation, but haven't yet invited law enforcement into their place. After some of that, we find ourselves parked at the front door, facing a large male in ripped up sweat shorts and a T-shirt emblazoned with an oversized Marijuana leaf.

He will not let us in.

A period of fruitless back and forth bickering follows. After a lot of hemming and hawing, I get what's going on. While Marijuana may be legal in Colorado, this guy's got other goodies in there he doesn't want a dog sniffing out.

I wait for a pregnant pause and say, "Sir, if we promised to limit our inquiry to just your boy and nothing else, would you grant us access?"

He stares at me, up and down. "You're that McMurtry gal, ain't ya?"

"Yes, sir, at your service. You can call me Jane if you prefer."

Dan shoots me a frown before his expression eases with appreciation for what I'm doing.

Still scanning me up and down, the father of the year asks, "You a cop?"

"No, sir. Just here to assist in finding your boy."

"Army reservist, right?"

"Yes, sir." I let that last "sir" sink hard. Treat them with respect even if they don't deserve it, Dad used to say, and they'll give you the foothold you're after.

"Alright," the guy says. "But only you come

in. No dogs."

Before all my colleagues go a cackling again, I rush to say, "How about it, Lieutenant? I go in, look for a better marker, check out the boy's room for clues, go from there."

Now it's the Lieutenant and I locked in a staring contest. He relents first. "OK."

"You sure about this?" Cassandra whispers next to me. "I don't like that guy." Next to her, Dan is nodding with more or less the same concern.

"Me neither," I whisper. "But he wants his boy bad enough to call in the cops, even when it could crash down on him. That's something to build on." I look over at Dan. "Besides, I ain't had a proper meal since yesterday afternoon, and I'm ready to be done with this so I can find a Denver omelet I'm hankering for."

I go inside, and Dad closes the door. Mom is sobbing quietly in one corner. Times like this call for quick and to the point verb and action, so I just get to it.

"Anything missing that your boy might have

taken?" I ask.

"What?" he says, almost in a shout.

"Tell you what, sir. I'm going to go into the boy's room, see if I can find a dirty, worn T-shirt, and meanwhile, you'll be looking through your valuables. See if any of it is missing."

"What are you getting at?"

"What I'm getting at is that a boy runs out with one of your... things." I cross my arms over my chest to act out how the boy might have done it. "What I'm getting at is that if you have another *thing* just like it, we'll wrap a dirty T-shirt on it for a minute or so, then you put your thing away, and I walk out with the T-shirt for my dogs to sniff. Sound like a plan?"

From the way he's looking at me, I wonder if I just said all that in Mandarin. "I'm looking for a scent of your boy with the thing he may have taken."

"OK," he says with a frown that suggests he's inching up to the edge of understanding, but a little more time is required for full dawn to break through.

"Boy's room this way?" I ask, though knowing where the alleged escape window is located, I don't need directions.

"Yeah. But wait. Let me go in there first."

"Sure thing." I squeeze to the side and let him by, and I just got the full picture.

He goes in and from the kitchen area where I'm now standing I hear him thrashing in there. In here, the mother goes on sobbing. I want to say something comforting, like hey, look on the bright side, at least you're not in Afghanistan getting shot up in your hut while your kids go missing in the nearby hills. But I doubt that would come across as terribly encouraging.

"How long did you say you needed to wrap the T-shirt?" the guy shouts out.

I look at my watch. "You doing it now?" When he grunts back in the affirmative, I say, "Let me time it." I wait for one minute by my watch, then tell him we're good. That's about the amount of time the kid would have had it as he tip-toed his way out of this tin can.

Dad comes out with the T-shirt. I think about

asking him whether his *thing*, a brick of Cocaine or a bag of Meth, I'm guessing, is missing. But the look on his face more than answers that for me.

"Thank you," I tell him.

"You think this will help you find him now?"

"No promises, but I'm expecting it will do a hell of a lot better than the teddy bear."

Mom sobs a little louder at that.

I walk out, T-shirt in hand and without wasting any time, I bring it to my dogs. They sniff it with relish and look up at me to let me know they're good to go. And we set off. We start at the mobile home's door and start tracing a route that takes us along a narrow trail, now illumined with early morning sunshine. Out of the corner of my eye, I see the news vans, two of them now. A female reporter and her camera man start following us on our left flank.

Cassandra mutters something, but I raise my hand to stop that. Here, on trail, it's about the dogs and the kid they're seeking.

The dogs are pulling fast. Cassandra holds Shady and follows me when the trail goes too narrow. Shadow pulls me ahead, and I let him. In the moment my chest fills up with pride and maybe a hint of hope. He's doing it. I'm doing it. We're doing it together.

Up a ways, in the direction the dogs are pointing, the trail winds through level ground. A bridge crosses over a dry creek, and that turmoil I felt earlier in my stomach returns threatening to snuff out that glimmer of hope I felt seconds ago. I feel dizzy for a moment.

I pull on Shadow's leash and slow down. Shady bumps against the back of my left prosthetic leg, nearly upending me with her own kind of clipping tackle.

"Sorry," Cassandra says. She comes alongside me and lowers her voice. "What's up?"

I don't know what's up or what's down. Or I don't want to say it. I only see another bridge and another creek. I can picture where this might end, and I don't want to go there. My head replays the image of a bloody girl's body, strewn unkindly against cold boulders while Shady howls next to it. All that I needed, I reproach myself. More bloody memories to freeze me in place. More flashbacks inside of flashbacks.

"You OK?" Cassandra presses me.

"Let her go."

"You sure?"

"Send her. I want her to find him."

Cassandra unclips Shady's leash and commands her to go. Without hesitation, she traces a straight line for the wooden bridge and scampers around it to go down. This time she doesn't run on the creek. She's under the bridge, and in another second I hear a young voice scream.

"Shady, Sit!" I command. I repeat that twice as Cassandra, Shadow and I run down trail.

We get to the bridge and I hand Shadow off to Cassandra and tell her, "Stay here, don't let anyone go down until I'm done."

I crawl down on my behind. When I get

there, I see Shady in a sitting position. I follow the line her nose is tracing, and I see him, wedged between a supporting beam and the sloping ground.

"Hey!" I say. "How are you doing?"

"Does he bite?" he asks.

"Nah. Only when I tell her. She's a girl dog, though. Gets a little upset when people call her a he."

He almost smiles at that. I get closer to see a bruise over his left eye, and a trickle of dried blood from a scratch along his left cheek.

"You OK?" I ask.

He shrugs.

"What's your name?"

"David."

"Hey, you know what, David? Lots'a people up there worried about you. How about you come out and we go see the sunrise, maybe get you a square breakfast."

He shakes his head. "He's going to kill me."

Though I know who he means, I side-step it with, "Your Mom and Dad are really worried about you. They'll be really glad to see you. Come on, let's go see 'em."

He shakes his head again. "They took it from me. They beat me and they took it."

I come closer and lower my voice. "No one needs to know about that. And your dad won't care neither. He's really scared about you." I'm trying hard to believe that last bit, once more banking on how the dad chanced getting busted by calling the cops, even if that was before he knew part of his inventory had gone missing.

"Wait here," I say. "Shady will keep you safe."

Up top I find the police contingent, blocked from further progress by Cassandra and Shadow, and none too happy about it.

"He's down there," I say. "A little scratched up, but OK. I need the dad." I look up and catch the big guy in the T-shirt not far away. I wave to him, foregoing asking for permission. "Your little boy is really scared," I say loudly for everyone's benefit. "Need you to calm him down."

Before anyone has much chance to object, I grab Shadow's leash. In another instant Dad, Shadow and I are making our way down. Under the bridge I put one hand on the guy's chest.

"Let's get something crystal, here, between you and me," I whisper. "You won't beat him up, and you'll take all that crap out of your house. Jesus, what the hell do you think you're doing?"

He's frowning at me. Shady picks up on his demeanor and lets out a growl. So does Shadow. Here, underneath this bridge, their growls echo with a hint of the sinister, and the semi-darkness around us only adds to that mood.

I do my own kind of growling. "I say the word, and all this turns out into an orange suit and a not so nice stay behind bars for you."

"I get that." He steps back and folds his arms.

"So then?"

"OK," he says.

"OK, what?"

"I won't take it out on him. I'll store my stuff

elsewhere."

We stare at each other, and for all that I don't like about this guy, I see sincerity there, like I would in a mean nasty dog that still retains a noble streak, especially when it comes to protecting his own.

I extend my hand. "Deal?"

"Deal," he says as we shake.

I let him take his boy first, and I follow with my dogs. A few minutes later, sitting in his car, I'll tell Dan what I did. He's not dumb. He'd pretty much figured it out from the second I asked to step into that mobile home.

"That's kind of how it is, ain't it Dan? Never clean. Never neat. Always feeling incomplete, unresolved, and unfulfilled. Or unfulfilling, whichever the case may be."

"Like those two wars you and Shadow witnessed."

"Yeah, like them. Except witnessed ain't the right word."

"Nah, I guess it's not," he says. "But at least we got a live one this time. You should be proud of that. You did good. Way more than just a tracker. You figured it out *and* you solved it. In some places they call that investigating."

"I reckon one could see it that way. Yeah, a live one this time. Let's see how much time it takes for him to turn into a dead one or one that brings death."

Dan pats me on the forearm. "You did good, Jane. Take that with you and nothing else."

We sit in silence for a few minutes. I'm spacing out, not thinking about much of anything.

"You took care of that other thing?" I ask.

"Your boss?"

"Yeah, him who shall remain nameless."

"Almost done. Shouldn't take long."

I look at Dan and force a smile. "Thank you."

He doesn't smile back. His eyes narrow, and I wonder what he sees in mine.

Chapter 18

"That is one creepy story," Allison says.

We're sitting in front of my living room TV, watching the morning shows. I'm not much of a news person, figuring I've seen enough carnage and tragedy up close and personal. I don't need to get a version of reality that comes at you in distilled, culled bite-sized factoids that seldom if ever represent how this world and its people thrash one another.

But today I'm not in a talking mood, and since I've noticed Allison's verbal productivity diminishes when doused with TV imagery, especially of the news kind, here we sit.

"You said that gal, Cassandra took Shadow in for a check at the base?" Allison asks.

"Yeah," I reply, worrying that perhaps we're about to venture into non-news territory I rather not cover.

However, with ardent waving she returns her attention to the TV. "Look at that. Those creeps were doing that same thing, killing kids, wrapping them with IEDs over in Afghanistan. Then they come home, do it some more here, off themselves, somehow do it so their bodies can't be found, and schedule-post a manifesto on their blog, with cross-linked posts to Twitter and Facebook. How twisted is that?"

"War is hell," I say.

She's aims the remote and uses it to mute the TV. "I know it's hell, but—"

"It twists people something fierce." I look at her. "I came back pretty twisted, Allison. Wrapped many times around. No one comes back untouched. You hear a story here or there on the news about PTSD, and wounded warriors, but it all sounds almost benign. It's not that way for us, for all of us coming back. We're all ruined six ways to Sunday, and then seven more."

"OK, but I'm pretty sure you're not saying what those guys did—"

"There, but for the grace of God, go I. Ever hear that one?"

"Yeah. Once or twice, but—"

"You're right. What they did ain't right. Not even close. Blackest of the black. But I've seen black, too, Allison. I haven't done it, but I've been on the edge. We all got it inside us, and the closer we get to war and other traumatic situations, the more we flirt with it."

She stops arguing with me, like she has in the past, when we get to talking about faith, and God, we come to an area where we disagree, and she doesn't want to turn over-the-top contentious. We have that arrangement, an unspoken one. She stops talking about it, and I drop it, though I don't know why or how she accepts it, because it usually gives me the last word.

After watching the story for a few more minutes, she turns off the TV. "Alright, they're just in a do-loop now," she says. "Annoying, non-informative," she adds in a singsongy tone. "Hey, so tell me more about that Dan guy. You two? You know…"

"We're cordial."

"Oh, yeah?" She cocks her head and pushes up one eyebrow.

"Dan's a busy guy. We live far away."

"An hour's far away? Too busy? You're going to have to do better than that."

"We're taking it slow. Like everybody should before they have kids, then waste a ton-load on a wedding, only to spend another ton-load on divorce lawyers. Life ain't no microwave. Breathe, take your time, think it through, do it in the right order."

"So, there's talk of marriage."

"Who said that?"

"You."

"I said no such thing. All's I said is we're taking it slow. Dan's finishing his PhD this semester. Between that and chasing bad guys, he's barely got time to pee."

Allison's about to say something clever, I'm sure, when my cellphone rings. It's Dan, who else. I answer it, my bad that I mention his name. I go in the kitchen, but when I look over my shoulder, Allison's standing on the doorway, one arm propped against it, her face going all goofy on me.

"Yeah, I saw it," I say when he asks me what I thought about the news story. "They covered it well," I add, choosing my words carefully. By covered I don't mean the usual news coverage sense, but rather how someone concealed Brady's tracks.

"By the way, Allison's here, says hi," I rush to add.

"Alright, so you're not free to talk, then," he notes.

"Not really. And we shouldn't now, anyway. But maybe over lunch or dinner sometime?" Now I make my own kind of goofy face at Allison.

He says he'll check his schedule and get back to me, and we hang up.

Allison comes over, her hand raised. "Up top, girl."

I humor her, and we laugh.

She turns to go back into the living room, then turns back to me. "Oh, I've been meaning to tell you." She makes another face and twirls her finger in a circular manner. "Remember those files I told you I lost that one time, back at the lab?"

"Yeah," I say, making an immediate connection to the MRI files of Shadow's hip.

"Well, my clever IT guy, without me asking, went in and did some... what did he call it? Oh, yeah. Low level forensic recovery. At the sector level or something. I think he's trying to impress me."

"Well, did he?"

"Oh, please. Geeks. Still, to his credit, here I'm thinking he's a lazy looser, and he blows me over with some actual initiative. Any-who, I got the files back, which I'm really stoked about because I took a closer look, and they have some interesting stuff."

"Wow. Good for you," I say, wavering on whether I really mean it.

"Maybe when you have some free time you can come by and take a look. I mean if it's not too boring for you. I know you're not much into science and stuff, but I think you'll really want to see this one file in particular."

"Yeah, sure. I can try the geek thing."

"Rock on, then." She raises her hand. "Up top, girl geeks unite."

I grin and give her another high five.

As she prepares to leave, Allison reaches into her purse and hands me a magazine. It's dog-tagged at page 21. She waves for me to open it, and when I do, I find a computer disc taped to the page.

I find a notepad and tear a page. On it I write, "How many copies?" In reply, she holds one finger.

With her purse still hanging from one shoulder, she follows me into the kitchen to watch me roll up the piece of paper and fire it up at one of the stove's burners. I let it burn until the flame hovers at my fingers, at which point I drop it into the sink. She comes over and with a hand on my back watches with me as the last of it turns to charcoal ash. I feel her hand rising and falling along my back as I turn on the faucet to wash the blackened blemish down the garbage disposal drain.

How I will use that disc or what role it will play in my future, I can't foresee. For now I know I'm glad to have it, and with the hug I give her as we part ways, I let Allison know I'm glad she gave it to me.

Staying in Touch

I hope you have enjoyed reading this story as much as I enjoyed writing it. If you would like to stay in touch with me and learn about future releases, join my reader's club at http://eduardosuastegui.com. From time to time, my newsletter will contain free downloads that I make available to my readers.

You may also send me an email with comments and feedback about this and other books at eswriting@gmail.com, or through my social media channels:

Twitter: http://twitter.com/eduardoauthor

Google+: http://plus.google.com/+EdSuastegui

You can learn more about writing at http://eduardosuastegui.com. Once there, I hope you browse through information about the *Our Cyber World* and *Tracking Jane* series.

Our Cyber World...
where cyber technology, artificial intelligence,
espionage, and electronic surveillance intersect.

Stories in this series…

Dead Beef

Pink Ballerina

Active Shooter

Decisive Moment

Beisbol Libre

Ghost Writer

*Random Origins***

*Feral***

*Semi**

*DroNET**

*Recombinant***

* Free when you join my mail list

** In work, to be released soon

Meet Major Jane McMurtry.
Her voice will draw you into her pain.
Her struggle will show you how to overcome.
In her search for love you will find hope.

Stories in this series…

Waiting for Shadow

Shadow-7

Rover

Fleeting Shadow *

Tahoe-1

Brownie

Blood Track

Heart Track**

* Free when you join my mail list

** In work, to be released soon